ETERNAL MAGIC

Dragon's Gift: The Huntress Book 4

Linsey Hall

CHAPTER ONE

"Oh no." I almost groaned when I caught sight of the golden sphinx crouched in front of the pyramid a hundred yards away. "It's a sphinx."

"Twenty bucks he has a riddle for us," Del said.

"Yep. And I'm terrible at riddles."

An enormous Egyptian pyramid stuck out of the desert like a sore thumb, the only thing for hundreds of miles. An ocean of sand rolled around us, hills and valleys stretching far into the distance. I'd lost track of how long we'd spent bouncing along on our camels.

Del tugged the brim of the hat over her forehead and muttered, "You're lucky I love you, Cass. Because of all the places for the dampening charm to be, it ended up in the middle of a freaking oven that blocks my magic."

I made a noise somewhere between a laugh and a moan. Sweat dripped down my back, and my own hat was doing a miserable job of keeping my nose from burning.

"I actually quite like Aladdin." I patted my camel's neck. He snorted, no doubt unimpressed by the name I'd bestowed upon him.

Normally, Del would use her powers as a transporter to teleport us straight to our desired destination. This pyramid, however, had been built by supernaturals in a weird part of the Sahara that blocked teleporting. It also blocked humans from getting near the pyramid, which was a small mercy considering that human archaeologists would definitely set off the magical booby traps inside.

No one wanted that. Not the archaeologists, who'd have their perception of reality rocked by the magic, and not the supernaturals, who tried to stay hidden from them.

Best to leave it to professionals like us.

"This is going to be some seriously old-school tomb raiding," I said to Del.

"No kidding. Riding a camel across the Egyptian desert in order to break into a pyramid is pretty much the height of cliché for a treasure hunter."

"I'll take it. The cliché stuff is sometimes the coolest. It's cliché for a reason, right? Everyone wants to do it." And even if it wasn't cool, I *really* wanted that dampening charm. I'd have ridden a yak a thousand miles through the tundra to get my hands on it, so a camel through the desert was no problem. I had plenty of incentive.

Victor Orriodor, the monster from our past hunted us. One day soon, we'd clash for good. I'd accepted it. Del, Nix, and I had concealment charms that hid us from him, but mine was faulty because of my new nullification power.

Which meant the time for running was almost over. We were at the point of kill or be killed. I planned to do the killing. But I had to get my powers back first or I'd never survive the confrontation.

I hoped the dampening charm would be the way to do that.

We were only a hundred yards from the pyramid now, close enough that I could make out the features of the golden sphinx who guarded the exit. His face was human, his body that of a lion's. He glittered in the sunlight almost like gold.

"He looks 3rd millennia BC," Del said. "They're usually the toughest to—"

She gasped as the sphinx lunged into the air and bounded across the sand toward us, his enormous stone body moving as if it were made of flesh and blood. Sand kicked up behind him as his powerful legs dug into the ground.

"Oh, hell." I tightened my grip on Aladdin's reins. Normally we'd approach, wake the sphinx up by tripping a lever or something, then answer the riddle to get through.

But this guy was gung ho. That was never good. It was the lazy temple guardians you wanted, if you had a choice.

He landed in front of us with a thud, his massive leonine body looming overhead. I tilted my head back, nearly blinded by his brightness.

"Holy magic," I breathed. He really *was* made of gold. I'd thought it a trick of the bright sun, but no. He was one hundred-percent, Grade-A golden goodness.

Covetousness welled in my heart, a greed so fierce that my fingers itched to pet the sphinx and coo *nice kitty*. Then tie him up and stick him in my trove.

Del and I were FireSouls, supernaturals believed to share the soul of a dragon. Like dragons, we had a thing for treasure. My idea of treasure was normally weapons and leather goods, but I could make an exception for a giant hunk of gold.

I shook my head, trying to focus on our reason for being here.

"What is your purpose?" he boomed.

I dragged my gaze away from the shining sphinx and looked at Del, whose eyes were wide as saucers.

"To take you home," she said breathlessly.

"Del!" I hissed. "Get ahold of yourself!"

Though I wasn't much better off. I may have lost my FireSoul powers last week, but I still seemed to possess the covetousness.

"Yeah, yeah," Del muttered, her gaze vacant. "I'm fine. It's just...shiiiny kitty."

"Kitty?" the sphinx boomed.

Oh, hell. We were screwed.

I'd have hoped an Egyptian sphinx wouldn't know the word for kitty, but he'd been enchanted to speak English, so he knew exactly what Del had called him.

The sphinx sat on his haunches and reached out with two massive paws, swooping us up, one in each paw. My head spun as we dangled in our smooth, hard cages. Shit. There was no way to budge a monster made of metal.

"Sorry!" I shouted. "You're not a kitty! You're a sphinx!"

"Yeah, a real badass sphinx!" Del yelled, struggling to break the sphinx's grip. "Toughest one I ever met!"

If I hadn't lost my powers last week, I could be out of here in a flash. I wouldn't use my lightning, because it'd go straight through the metal and fry me, too, but I could use my illusion power to scare the crap out of him so he'd drop us.

Unfortunately, none of that was an option now.

In a fight last week, I'd acquired the power to nullify other supernaturals' abilities. Because I was a FireSoul, I could steal other people's powers. I hadn't wanted to take that cursed power, but it'd been the only way to prevent catastrophe. As a result, my new nullification power canceled out my innate powers. I'd been a mess ever since it had happened, and I hated it, but that didn't mean I wouldn't try to use it.

The sphinx shook us. My brain felt like it rattled in my head. I closed my eyes and tried to ignore it, focusing on my new gift, which was a weird kind of non-magic. that canceled out other supernaturals' magical gifts.

The strain of trying to manipulate the unfamiliar magic broke sweat across my skin. I'd been practicing my new power, but hadn't made much progress. I felt only emptiness within, an uncomfortable feeling of nothingness that rolled in my stomach like hunger and queasiness combined.

I gave up and shouted, "Del! Use your phantom power!"

"Right! Of course!" Her bright gaze drifted back to the golden sphinx. "Just a bit distracted, is all."

"Come on!"

She shook her head violently as if to clear it. Though my FireSoul liked gold, Del's loooooved it. It was a dangerous, but unavoidable, weakness.

Del's magic surged on the air, her signature distinct. The scent of fresh laundry and the feel of soft grass beneath my feet were a delight compared to the hot, hard grip of the sphinx.

Her skin shimmered as she turned a transparent blue, and her black hair became a silvery indigo. When she'd gone full phantom-ghosty, she slipped from the sphinx's grip and landed on the sand.

The sphinx roared, the noise pounding my eardrums. I winced.

He swatted at Del with his free paw, but it sailed right through her.

Del drew her sword. The blade flared a fiery cobalt. Whenever Del was in phantom form, the objects she touched took on the properties of a phantom.

"Get ready to run!" She turned corporeal for a second, swinging her now solid steel blade at the sphinx's haunches.

It bounced off with a clang and she cursed. The sphinx batted her away with a paw, clearly more annoyed than angry. She landed on her butt in the sand.

"I don't think I can get you out of this, Cass," Del said.

Damn.

"We're just visiting," I said. "How do we pass?"

The sphinx looked at me, his massive nose level with mine.

"A riddle," he said.

Of course.

"It accepts the blind and grants them sight."

Uhhh… My brain blanked. I glanced at Del. She shrugged.

"Can I get a clue?" I asked.

"No."

"Phone a friend?"

The sphinx shook me. "Wrong!"

"A moment! Just a moment!" I shouted.

He stopped shaking. I pressed my fingertips to the golden charm hanging at my throat, igniting the magic that fueled the communications spell.

"Nix?" I said. "You there?"

"Yeah. What do you need?"

"Thank magic." Nix was Del's and my other half—other third?—and she was my phone-a-friend when on tomb-raiding jobs. Riddles were surprisingly common, and I was awful at them. Normally, I worked alone so I needed the help, though Del had come along on this job because I could no longer use my dragon sense to find things, and I needed her to use hers to lead us to the dampening charm.

"Got a riddle for you," I said as the sphinx glowered. His fist tightened on my ribs, and I saw stars. When it loosened a bit, I gasped out the riddle to Nix.

"Takes the blind and grants them sight?" Nix asked. "Oh jeez, that's tough. Let me Google it."

The clickity-click of her keyboard keys sounded through the charm. The sphinx shook me.

"Hurry up, Nix!" I shouted. My ribs felt like they were grinding together.

"Hang on, hang on, I'll get it!"

I wished we weren't treasure hunters who had to rely on Google, but there you had it. It was the modern age. What job *didn't* rely on Google?

The sphinx tightened his grip slightly. "Answer!"

"Nix!"

"Uh, uh." The keyboard clickity-clicked. "School! It's a school!"

"School!" I shouted. "A school takes the blind and makes them see! It, uh, gives them knowledge to understand and see the world around them." Right? For magic's sake, I hoped it was right.

"Correct." The sphinx nodded.

I sagged in relief. "So I'm good? You'll let us pass?"

"Yes. But you must find your own way into the temple."

"Fair enough." I'd hoped he'd tell us how to get in, but as long as he wouldn't eat me, I'd be happy.

"But hurry. I grow hungry."

I nodded frantically and saluted. "Aye-aye."

The sphinx's grip loosened, and I slipped right out, my way no doubt hastened by the sweat slicking my skin. When I tumbled to the sand, the stuff stuck to every inch of exposed skin and snuck inside my clothes.

I clambered to my feet, wishing I were incorporeal like Del, and then struggled onto Aladdin. All while still covered in sand.

Life without my powers sucked.

Del climbed onto her camel, who I'd dubbed Jasmine because she had nicer eyelashes than Aladdin, and we flicked the reins, the camel version of cranking the key in the ignition.

"Come on, Aladdin!" I shouted.

Aladdin picked up the pace, galloping across the sand toward the pyramid in the distance. I bent low over his back, trying not to bounce off. My camel-riding skills were seriously rusty, and his gait wasn't exactly smooth. More drunken horse than racehorse.

I glanced back over my shoulder to see the sphinx watching us, but he hadn't followed. When I turned back, we were nearly to the pyramid. It was massive, the stones in far better condition than if this had been a human-built pyramid. Spells protected it, slowing decay and destruction.

We pulled Aladdin and Jasmine to a stop at the base of the pyramid. I hopped off, then pulled a big water bottle from the saddlebag. Del did the same. I unscrewed the top and held the bottle up for Aladdin.

He plucked it right out of my hand and held it in his front teeth, then tipped his head back and drank. His floppy lips quivered in delight.

"Looks like you've got that under control." I patted him on the shoulder. "Be back in a bit. Don't litter."

I turned to see Jasmine snatch the water bottle out of Del's hand.

"I like these camels." Del grinned as she slung her bag crosswise over her back and turned to face the pyramid. "Let's find a way in."

"This has got to be the front since it was the side the sphinx was guarding, but I don't see an entrance." The side of the pyramid was smooth and sloped, not the stepped construction of the Mayan pyramids in Mexico.

"There." Del pointed to a spot about ten feet above our heads. "See the indented spot? About the size of a door?"

"Yeah." I squinted. "There's no lever or any other way to trigger the door."

"Nope," Del said. "Probably only accessible if you know the right spell."

No wonder the sphinx had let us go so easily. There was no easy way in. I glanced back over my head at the sphinx.

His head swung to look at me, as if he sensed my gaze. He stood and began to slink toward us, his gait now predatory. Stalking.

I turned back to Del, my heart suddenly pounding. "He's coming to eat us."

She looked warily at the sphinx. "Yeah? But he let us go."

"It was all a game." Which I should have guessed. "He'd known we couldn't get in and had planned to chomp us all along, but he wanted to play with his prey first."

Del nodded, her wide gaze stuck on the sphinx. "He *is* a cat. And he looks hungry."

I frowned as I studied the door above. "There might be an escape lever inside. Something to trigger it from within."

"Of course. Only accessible to those worthy enough to get in in the first place."

They'd never expected a supernatural like Del to show up one day. She was one of a kind, the only person I'd ever heard of who walked the line between life and death. Half phantom, half human. And she was the ace up our sleeve. "You're going to have to pull your phantom trick, Del."

She nodded. "Yeah. I got it."

Little notches in the sloped stone wall caught my eye. I pointed them out to Del. "There. That's how we climb. You go first."

I followed Del up the wall, my belly flat against the stone and my fingertips clinging to the little indents. Sweat dripped down my spine as we scaled the side of the pyramid. Every time I glanced over my shoulder, the sphinx lurked closer.

One time, he was licking his golden chops. My heart raced, and sweat rolled down my spine. Even my FireSoul didn't want to spend eternity in a golden sphinx's belly.

When she reached the indent, Del's magic surged as she turned into a phantom and slipped through the wall.

The desert was suddenly a lot quieter without her. I could hear the wind whipping my hair away from my face and feel the sun pounding on the back of my neck.

A quick look over my shoulder revealed the sphinx only a couple dozen yards away. He was close enough for me to make out the details of his face, and boy, were his fangs long.

"Come on, Del," I muttered.

A grinding noise sounded, and I turned away from the sphinx. The indented entrance stone was moving backwards, disappearing into the pyramid.

I scrambled up to the ledge as the stone slid toward the right, into an indent in the wall. A dark corridor stretched ahead, a cool gust of wind blowing out. It smelled dusty and old, and I wondered how long it had been since someone had come in here.

Probably millennia. Ever since the original builders had died out.

I shivered, but not from cold.

It was eerie.

The stone disappeared entirely into the wall on my right, revealing Del, who was once again corporeal. I walked farther into the tunnel, glancing back to see an enormous golden eye staring in from the exit.

I waved at the sphinx, who growled, then turned to Del and raised my hand. The magic in my lightstone ring flared to life, shedding a golden glow over the dark tunnel. It sloped down, into the depths of the massive structure.

"Ready?" Del asked.

"As I'll ever be."

Del turned to start down the corridor as my light glinted off a razor wire stretched at neck level right ahead of her.

"Stop!" I lunged for her and grabbed the bag strapped to her back, dragging her to a halt. She stopped abruptly.

"Razor wire." I raised my light to shine on it, but the wire was imperceptible again. It was only visible in the perfect light from the perfect angle. I pulled Righty, one of my trusty daggers, from my thigh sheath and held it out, waving it slowly till it tapped against the wire. "Thin enough you can't see it most times. I got lucky with the lightstone."

"Yeah." A shuddery breath escaped Del. "I forgot about those. I've read how the Egyptians liked them for booby-traps, but completely forgot."

"It's cool. You don't do this as much as me. Too busy killing demons."

"True. But I'm glad you've got my back," Del said.

Most of the time, Del was a bounty hunter who worked on commission for the Order of the Magica, the government body overseeing all magic users. They'd toss her in jail if they knew she was a FireSoul, totally uncaring that she'd never use her abilities to kill and steal another Magica's powers. Getting tossed in the Prison for Magical Miscreants was pretty much all our worst nightmares.

Fortunately, the Order didn't bother communicating directly with lowly bounty hunters. She never had to come into direct contact with them.

"I'll lead." I shined my light ahead and held Righty out at neck level, hoping it would catch on a wire before it could slit my throat.

It caught on three, and I was grateful as hell each time. As we walked, we passed by walls painted with tall, elegant figures. This would have been a burial place for a king or queen, the paintings telling the story of their life. Every now and then, statues stood lined up along the wall, ancient figures who'd been guarding this passage for millennia.

I'd have liked to have spent more time looking, but I wanted to get my hands on the dampener charm and see if it worked to suppress my nullifying powers enough that my normal gifts could be used.

We came to a split in the path, one leading down and the other continuing up.

"What do you think?" I asked Del. I wished I could use my own dragon sense to determine the way, but that wasn't an option until I got the charm.

She closed her eyes, and her magic swelled on the air, the scent of clean cotton driving away the dusty aroma.

"Both could possibly work, but I think up," she said.

"Up," I said. "More important royalty were buried higher in the pyramid, so I bet it's the shorter route."

"Agreed."

We veered right and started up the sloped path. After a few yards, the ground ahead turned white.

"Weird," I said. A thick powder coated the entire path for the next several yards.

Del grabbed my shoulder, and I jerked to a halt.

"Retreat," she whispered. "Don't breathe."

The seriousness in her voice froze my muscles. I stopped breathing and stepped back. We turned and hurried away.

When we reached the crossroads where we'd split off, I gasped in a breath and asked, "What was that?"

"Hematite powder. It's super tiny granules but super sharp. If it gets into our lungs, it'll kill us slowly."

"Ouch." Slow death was a big no-go area in my life plan. "Okay. Let's go down and see if we can get around."

We followed the sloped path down, checking out two false chambers on the way. Both had contained boxes full of treasure, but not the dampener charm. I'd seen diagrams of pyramids in which there were chambers deep under the desert. I was starting to lose track of how deep we'd gotten, but it felt like we'd left reality behind. It was deadly silent, dark, and the place shimmered with all kinds of threatening magic.

The air became more stale and the feel of the magic stronger as we descended. Supernaturals could usually only feel other living supernaturals' signatures. But this place was different, and in all likelihood, haunted.

"I think the booby traps are about to get a lot harder," I muttered.

"Yep."

A moment later, the path opened up into a room. It was mostly empty with the exception of a statue of a seated god. The body was human, the head that of a jackal.

"Anubis," Del said. "God of the dead."

Around him, the walls were decorated with hieroglyphs. Every inch of stone was carved to tell a story that I couldn't interpret.

"The door will be behind Anubis," I guessed.

We approached slowly, our footsteps silent on the stone floor. I kept my gaze trained on Anubis's face, waiting for any sign of life. Just because he was stone now didn't mean he wouldn't hop up and curse us.

I was so intent on his face that I almost missed the hieroglyph to the left side of his head starting to glow. It looked like a bird, which could mean just about anything. The symbol shined bright, then peeled itself away from the wall.

It shot toward us, quick as flame, and I threw myself to the side, pushing Del out of the way. As it flew by, the magic smelled like decay. Sick and dark.

"Curses!" I said. "Don't let them hit you."

There was no way to fight cursed hieroglyphs. Swords would do nothing, and neither of us had any kind of manipulation magic. If that would even work. If they hit us, they'd impart whatever curse they carried.

I did *not* want one of those.

Another glowing hieroglyph shot from the wall. I lunged left, avoiding it by a hair's breadth.

Shit, shit, shit.

I called upon my nullification power, praying that it would work. Disempowering the magic that fueled the hieroglyphs was our only hope.

Normally, my innate magic felt distinct—the burn of flame or the chill of ice. But the nullification power felt like nothing. I reached for it anyway, praying I could get ahold of it and actually use it to my advantage.

On a stretch of mad luck, the nullification power surged, making my insides hollow out. I envisioned the cursed hieroglyphs falling to the ground and disappearing.

Two of them did just that, their glowing forms fizzling out as my nullification power dampened their magic. The dampening charm we were looking for was similar to my new power. But I hoped to use it *against* my new power.

Del looked around warily. "I think you've done it."

"Yeah. Don't know why it worked this time when it didn't with the sphinx."

"Practice, maybe."

I glanced around warily, in case any other curses decided to jump off the wall. "I don't think so. I never feel like I'm in control. Sometimes it works, sometimes it doesn't." And I'd never been very successful with the few times I'd tried to practice.

"Well, whatever it is, let's get out of here before you can't hold them at bay."

"Agreed."

We walked to Anubis and peered around the back of his stone chair. There was a small passage. The exit was so easy. There wasn't even a door. I swallowed hard, shivering.

"If it's this easy to get out, those curses we dodged were definitely deadly," I said. They'd planned to drop us in our tracks before we could even hope to get through this unguarded exit.

"Yep." Del ducked and went through.

I followed, holding my light out ahead.

The passage on the other side was narrower than the one we'd been traveling down, but we could at least stand upright.

"It leads up," Del said.

I raised my ring to reveal the path that tilted sharply upward. "We're getting close."

I led the way up the path, keeping my light and my blade raised high to find any razor wires.

"Watch the ground at my feet," I said, thinking back to a time five years ago when Del and I had been raiding a tomb in Southeast Asia. I hadn't watched the ground ahead and had almost fallen into a pit of spiders. Del had caught me just in time, but I didn't want to count on her doing it again.

Fortunately, she didn't find any trap holes, and I didn't fall into any. By the time we reached the room at the end of the hall, I was vibrating with the tension of waiting for the next booby-trap.

"This is weird," Del said.

I looked at the piles of wood that were laid out neatly on the floor. Coils of rope were piled next to the wood. The walls were decorated with carved reliefs and hieroglyphs, but no door.

"Yeah," I said. "Definitely odd."

"At least the hieroglyphs aren't coming alive," Del said.

"Small mercies. But I don't know what the hell we're supposed to do with this wood."

"Light a fire?"

I looked up, searching for holes in the wall. I caught sight of one in the ceiling. "Doubtful. There's only one small air shaft in here. A fire would suck up all the oxygen in a heartbeat."

I studied the carvings on the wall. There were hundreds, every inch covered with a story I couldn't decipher. Del paced the edges of the room.

"No hidden doors," she said.

My gaze roved the wall, looking for the beginning of the story. Maybe that would help me understand what we were supposed to do to get out of this weird room. The Egyptians wrote from right to left, in columns, so I started in the upper right corner of each wall.

"I can't find the start," I told Del.

"Well, it's about a boat." She pointed to one wall where a long, low boat was depicted on many of the carvings. Depending on the scene, the boat was loaded with goods or people. In the final scene, only one person rode upon the boat, standing at the bow.

I glanced at the piles of wood and rope. "Shit."

"What?" Del asked.

"We have to build the boat."

She laughed. "Build a boat?"

I crouched near one of the piles of wood while scouring the surface for clues. I found them near the edges of the wood. "Yeah. Look here. There's holes all along the edges of the wood. And these little dash marks near the edge are a key."

"A key?"

"Yep. We're basically working with eighteenth dynasty Ikea furniture here. The four dashes on this piece of wood correspond with the four dashes on that piece." I pointed to the long board right next to the one I was studying. "These two boards go next to each other. We just follow the directions. And the boards are jagged on the edges." They actually looked a bit like very fat lightning bolts rather than your normal rectangular boards. "So they kinda fit together like a puzzle anyway."

"Wow, you're right," Del said.

"Except we have no nails," I said. "Or a hammer."

Del's face lit up. "We don't need them. The Egyptians lashed their boats together with rope. I read that once."

I glanced at the coils of rope, the last piece of the puzzle and the one I hadn't quite understood. "Of course. There's the rope."

Del high-fived me. "Good work, Sherlock."

"Let's just hope we can build the thing."

"At least it's not a big boat," Del said.

"Just pray it's not a real river we're going to be traveling upon." But I didn't think so. I didn't see any caulking material, for one. And this was the desert. I'd bet money that the boat, when fully constructed, ignited a spell. We might travel down a magical river, but there'd be no real water.

"Let's get started then," Del said.

It took us a solid four hours and a whole lot of cursing, but we managed to get the small boat built. It was about twelve feet long and narrow. The jagged-edged planking had made it easier to assemble than I'd expected. Just like building a giant jigsaw puzzle. There were a few small spare chips of wood left over that we hadn't been able to figure out, but it looked like a boat.

To finish the job, we wedged some larger pieces of wood next to the curved bottom of the boat to keep it sitting upright. They were too bulky to be pieces of the boat, so we assumed that was their purpose.

We stood next to our creation, our hands on our hips.

"So now what?" Del asked.

"I guess we should get in it."

Gingerly, we climbed into the boat. As soon as my foot left the ground, the air shimmered with magic. It sparkled with a bright light and tingled against my skin.

In front of us, the ground turned to a shimmering blue, like a river. The boat moved, creaking forward on the river of magic.

Del gasped. I held on tight.

We drifted along the floor. When the bow touched the wall, I clenched my fists.

Come on.

The bow pierced the wall, gliding through effortlessly. The boat flowed forward. When I was nose to nose with the wall, I squeezed my eyes shut, unable to help myself.

When I didn't feel the rough scrape of stone on my nose or the feeling of being shoved backward, I opened my eyes.

And stared straight into the black gaze of a mummy. A golden mask of a bird was propped over his face, and thin strips of dusty white fabric wrapped around his whole body.

I shrieked and lunged left, tumbling out of the boat.

You've got to be kidding me. I'd raided over half a dozen pyramids and the mummy was never *awake*. I scrambled away from him, my frantic gaze taking in the elaborate furniture, the ornately decorated boxes, and the food that sat out on golden platters.

The mummy's sarcophagus sat in the center of the room, the heavy stone top pushed all the way off.

Del appeared as the boat finished drifting through. She screamed and tumbled out of the boat, too.

"He's not supposed to be awake!" she shouted as she crab-walked backward, away from the mummy.

His beaked face was turned toward her. I had no idea if there was a bird head in there, but I didn't want to find out.

He lumbered toward her, his arms outstretched. He moved slowly, in that comical way of old horror movies, but I'd heard mummies were damned strong if you had the misfortune to run across one who was alive.

"Gimme a sec! I'll figure it out!" Frantically, I searched the room, feeling out all the magical signatures.

I didn't want to hurt the mummy. Of all the historical treasures in this room, he was number one. And he was technically a person. Or he had been. Now he was a soul who couldn't cross over. But if I wasn't going to hurt him, I needed something to incapacitate him.

Egyptian royalty had traveled to the afterlife in their boat, like the one we'd ridden on, equipped with spells and magic that could ward off any bad things they might encounter on the other side.

There had to be something in here to help me.

"Cass! Hurry!" Del dodged the mummy, trying to stay out of his grasp.

There were weapons stacked against the walls, but she ignored them, likely knowing how much I wanted to avoid hurting him. I might raid tombs for a living, but I tried not to do much damage.

"Hold him off, Del," I yelled. "I'm working on it!"

I raced around the room, feeling out the magical signatures of the artifacts. Only some had power, but most were indecipherable. That was normal—I didn't usually even think about objects' signatures because I couldn't often tell what they were. But I needed abnormal now.

The mummy made a weird rasping noise as he chased Del. The sound made the hair on the back of my neck stand up.

"I think he's upset!" Del yelled.

"Yep!" I hesitated near a golden vial. The magic that radiated from it made my skin tingle.

I shook my head and moved on. Too much energy in that one.

"Watch out!" Del shouted.

I looked up. The mummy was coming straight at me, hands outstretched in classic mummy pose. It would have been funny if I weren't so freaked out.

I dodged to the left, but he grabbed my arm.

"Shit!" I tried to yank away, but his grip was strong as steel. And cold. Way too cold for a mummy in this heat. His black gaze burned into me as I pulled away. Before I raced across the room, I got a feel for his magic and caught the slightest whiff of decay. That scent usually accompanied dark magic. Beneath it was the smell of fresh fruit.

It hit me then. The mummy had been cursed. The fruity smell was his normal magic. The decay was the scent of the curse lingering over him. I'd smelled the like before, on people who were wearing slave collars that poisoned them with dark magic. Aaron, the only other

FireSoul I'd ever met besides my *deirfiúr*, had smelled like that.

The mummy made a rasping noise and whirled to face me.

"He's cursed," I said. "That's why he's awake."

"So let's put him to sleep."

The mummy lumbered toward us, creepy as hell with his dead-looking eyes peering out through the golden mask. Maybe I could nullify the curse that kept him awake.

"Distract him while I try something," I said.

Del gave a little whoop that attracted the mummy's attention. When his head swung toward her, she raced toward him, then dodged away. He followed.

I focused on the Nullifier's magic, trying to draw it out of myself and propel it toward the mummy.

But I got nothing but crickets. Whatever nullifying gift I had lay dormant inside me. Except for the fact that it screwed with my own magic.

Damn it.

"Find a charm or potion that might put him to sleep," I said. "There might be something here to help him in the afterlife."

Del and I began to search, feeling for the magical signature on the enchanted artifacts and potions. The mummy raced after us, hot on our heels as we dodged him.

I plucked a blue vial off the top of a box when the mummy's cold hand gripped my arm again. I yanked away, shuddering, and the desperate noise that rattled through his throat made my hair stand on end. I darted to the other side of the room, trying to focus on the feel of the magic in the blue vial I clutched.

A calm, relaxing magic emitted from it. The magic was hard to describe, but I'd bet this would do the trick.

"Help me lure him to the sarcophagus!" I called to Del.

"Hey, Boris!" she yelled, waving her arm. She stood behind the sacrocphogus, leaving me with the job of pushing him in.

Thanks, Pal.

The mummy whirled around, then stalked toward her. I raced after him. He veered around the sarcophagus, but I shoved him in, cringing when my hands met his cold wrappings.

His top half bent over the sarcophagus and he struggled.

"Ugh," I bent down and grabbled his cold legs, then tried to heave him up into the sacrocaphagus. "Little help, here!"

Del joined me and we heaved him into the big stone box. He thrashed and turned over.

"Hold him down!" I uncorked the bottle.

Del pressed on the mummy's shoulders, pinning him, and I held the vial over his beak, praying to magic that this would work.

There was a hole at the end of his beaked mask, so I poured the potion over the spot. The liquid was silvery and clear.

A second later, he calmed.

We stepped back, watching him warily.

"Feel better?" I asked.

He started to rise, and I stepped forward to push him back in. But his movements were so slow, and so indicative of someone who was tired, that I hesitated. He gestured to the room and all the treasure, then to me.

"What?" I asked.

He gestured again, pointing to a pile of gold and then to me.

"I can take some?" I asked, my FireSoul jumping in delight. Normally, I'd take stuff anyway, but I always returned it after we'd taken the magic charm from the artifact. But was he giving me permission?

That was a first.

The mummy nodded.

I smiled. "Thanks."

He lay back down, and a moment later, his magic disappeared and his limbs stilled.

He was asleep. Or dead. Whatever the case, he was happy about it.

Del slumped to the ground. "For magic's sake, that was weird."

"Yeah." Even my knees felt a little weak. I was used to spells and monsters and demons, but not mummies. They were parts of history. The idea of hurting one had freaked me the hell out.

That had been a close one.

I glanced around the room, finally able to take it all in. "Whoa."

"Yeah. This dude was loaded."

Furniture was everywhere, with gorgeous boxes filling in the rest of the space. In one corner was another pile of wood, no doubt the boat for the deceased. The dry air kept everything fairly well preserved, but magic was obviously playing a role, too. The food, set out thousands of years ago for him to take to the afterlife, was still fresh-looking.

"Can't believe that guy didn't mind that we take some of this stuff," Del said.

"I know. Easiest job we've ever done." Our shop, Ancient Magic, made its profit selling the magic encased in enchanted artifacts. With time, magic decayed and became unstable. If left to its own devices, it could cause some serious problems. Explosions, plagues, that kind of thing.

So we stuck to taking magic from the dangerously decayed artifacts, and we returned the original artifacts to their sites. We then put the magic in a replica and sold it. It kept us on the right side of the law and our consciences clear.

"Let's start by finding the dampening charm. Got a lead?" I asked Del.

She closed her eyes, no doubt focusing on her dragon sense. An ugly little twinge of jealousy hit me, but mostly it was a sense of loss. I'd only been without my powers for a week, and I was already flailing.

"That way." Del pointed toward the edge of the room near the mummy's feet. "In that small box on the floor, I bet."

I went to it and dropped to my knees.

"You do that," Del said. "I'm going to see if I can find a latch to open a door to get out of here. I don't think the boat will go back through the wall."

"Okay." I reached for the box. It was the kind that had a lot of little fasteners to open it. I worked at them, being as careful as I could.

There was a flash of golden light, then Del's exclamation. "Got it!"

I glanced up. She was standing near an arched gap in the wall. A door. Good.

I turned back to the box and opened it. A wide, gold bracelet sat on a bed of white cloth. I reached for the cuff. Torchlight glimmered on its shining golden surface, but it wasn't the gold that was so entrancing. It was the promise of its magic. If this worked, I'd have my powers back.

My fingers trembled as they grazed the smooth surface. I gripped it and picked it up, sliding it onto my wrist, where it sat, cool and heavy.

"Shit!" Del cried.

I whirled around.

Five demons had appeared, their burnished red skin gleaming in the torchlight. Small horns protruded from their heads, and their fangs peeked out from their upper lips. They were armed with flaming swords, and their magic smelled like a garbage fire.

Oh, we were screwed.

CHAPTER TWO

Where the hell had they come from? This place was blocked from transporting.

Unless they protected the treasure, and once I'd touched it, they'd been called? But we'd disturbed the pyramid's booby traps in other ways. I'd have thought they'd have come at that point.

Del's magic swelled, the fresh cotton scent drowning out the dusty aroma of the pyramid. Her skin glimmered blue, and she lit up the dim room, especially when she drew her sword, which glowed like cobalt flame.

She lunged for the nearest demon, going corporeal long enough to lop off his head before turning back into a phantom.

I called upon my magic, reaching deep within and praying that the dampening charm worked and I could access my innate gifts.

But I got nothing. Just the same familiar emptiness of my nullification magic. Disappointment welled as I yanked off the cuff.

I was about to shove it into my pocket when a demon appeared beside me. He sliced his blade toward me and I leapt back, but the tip of the sword caught on the cuff and knocked it out of my hand.

It flipped end over end, flying across the room to land in a far corner amongst some boxes.

I ignored it, lunging out of the demon's reach and grabbing the twin obsidian daggers strapped to my thighs. Looked like I'd be doing this the old-fashioned way.

The demon charged as I flung Righty at him. The black glass blade sunk into his eye. A horrific sound gurgled from his throat as he dropped where he stood, his fire-sword clattering to the ground and the flame dying. I hurried to him and crouched to pull the dagger out of his skull, gagging slightly at the squelchy noise. I wiped it on his shirt, then raced across the room to join Del.

She was whirling through the group of demons, a phantom dancer with deadly intent. Her blade moved fast as a whip, turning to steel long enough to sever limbs and pierce hearts.

Ever since she'd learned she was part phantom earlier this year, her deadliness with a sword had gone off the charts. She couldn't be killed while in phantom form, so she'd gotten even bolder with her moves. Demons dropped like flies, which was good, because they kept appearing out of thin air.

"Little help here!" Del called.

"On it!"

I flung Righty at a demon creeping up behind her. The blade pierced his chest. Before he even had a chance to fall, I nicked my finger with Lefty, using my blood to ignite the magic that connected the two daggers. Righty pulled itself out of the demon and flew back to me.

As much as I'd loved these blades back when I hadn't been able to use my magic, they now felt cumbersome and weak compared to my now-lost ability to shoot lightning from my fingertips.

Del and I set up a pattern, her taking the demons on one side of the room while I took the other. Our blades flashed in the torchlight, and we dodged the artifacts and treasures, not wanting to trample anything. The bastard demons didn't seem to care, though. They swung their fire swords with abandon.

And there were too many of them. They just kept appearing.

"We gotta run for it!" I glanced toward the corner where the dampening charm had fallen. It hadn't worked, and we were being overrun here. Leaving it was the best option.

"Agreed!" She lopped off one more head, then spun to charge the exit.

We raced through the room and down the corridor, occasionally turning when the sound of footsteps grew too close. I'd fling a dagger or Del would plunge her sword, but there'd always be one demon shortly behind the other.

My lungs burned with the strain as I pushed myself harder, trying not to lose my footing. The only way to escape these guys was speed, though I had no idea what we'd do when we reached the cursed hieroglyphs room. Try to outrun them, I guessed.

We were almost to the hieroglyphs room when a demon caught me by the collar, dragging me back.

I screamed as he raised his flaming sword over my head.

Get it together!

I dropped my weight hard to the floor. The demon stumbled, but his grip didn't loosen. I rolled, swiping out with my blade.

It cut deep into his forearm and blood spurted, spraying my face with warm wetness.

I gagged as his grip loosened, then yanked myself away and stumbled back. When I had enough room to move my arm, I flung Righty. The blade sunk into his chest, and he fell to his knees.

Behind him, two more demons raced toward us.

"On your left!" Del shouted.

I dodged, allowing her to race past me. She killed one demon with a powerful swipe across his jugular, but while she was corporeal, the other got her in the side with his blade.

She screamed and stumbled away. I flung Lefty, aiming for the demon's neck. It plunged in, and blood sprayed across the corridor.

As he fell, I raced to Del, who was leaning on the wall, her face drawn.

"You okay?" I pulled at her shirt, trying to see her wound.

"Yeah, yeah." She raised her shirt to reveal a shallow slice. "Just a little one. But damn, those fire blades hurt. Like, *incapacitate you* hurt."

"Yeah, probably to stun you while they go in for the kill."

"Bastards." She glared at the bodies on the ground.

They were already starting to disappear, returning back to their hell. That was the nice thing about demons—you didn't get the guilt of having actually killed them, and they cleaned themselves up once they were dead.

I glanced back down the corridor, but saw no more coming.

"Why aren't there anymore?" I asked. We hadn't passed any kind of threshold that would have stopped them, like sometimes happened with tomb guardians.

"Killed 'em all?"

"Maybe. But their numbers seemed pretty endless."

"Yeah, it is a bit weird that they stopped coming," she said. "But you got the dampening charm, right?"

"I grabbed it, but it didn't work. A demon knocked it out of my hand, and I didn't have time to get it back before we ran for it."

"Let's go get it."

"But it didn't work."

"You don't know. Maybe we need to do something with it. Ignite the magic or a spell. And we can get a few items for our shop, courtesy of our mummy friend."

"Good point. And maybe we can fix up some of the damage those damned demons did." I hated to leave an archaeological site worse than when I found it. It was irreparably altered, but maybe I could help a bit.

"Just keep an eye out for more demons," Del said. "They might reappear when we get back to the treasure room."

I nodded.

It didn't take us long to make our way back. With the door now open to the main treasure room, we didn't have to build any boats.

When we reached the entrance to the treasure room, we hesitated. Without a dozen demons with fire swords, it didn't look quite so bad. There were a few broken boxes and artifacts tumbled around, but for the most part, it looked almost whole.

"Keep watch," I said. "I'll find the dampening charm and some artifacts."

"'Kay." Del tugged the bag off her back and handed it to me. In her phantom form, she stepped into the room, her sword raised.

I went to the corner where the dampening charm had fallen. Ornate wooden boxes were stacked about waist high. I searched between them, finally spotting the glint of gold. I grabbed the cuff. When I pulled it out, I scowled at it and shoved it into my pocket.

"Sense anything particularly old?" I asked Del as I went to the center of the room.

She pointed to a box that had tumbled to the floor and broken open. "That guy feels almost expired."

I knelt at the box and immediately felt the magic. It pulsed strongly and smelled of turpentine. I turned the box upright, opened it, and peered inside.

Delicate white fabric was wrapped around an object about eight inches long. I pulled my phone from my pocket and snapped a pic, recording the wrapping style so that when I returned the artifact to the box after we'd taken the magic, I could wrap it up the same way. I should have done that with the dampening charm, but I'd lost my head a bit.

After setting the phone on my thigh, I peeled the fabric away. If this had been a human archaeological site, the fabric would be as fragile as a layer of dust. Unwrapping the artifact would have destroyed the fabric and possibly the artifact itself, depending on what it was made of.

But because the supernaturals who had built this pyramid had enchanted it against decay, I had a lot more freedom in my work.

The fabric fell away to reveal an alabaster statue of Bastet, the Egyptian cat god. The magic pulsed even stronger when I held the alabaster against my skin, but I couldn't quite identify it.

I snapped another picture of the statue in front of the box so that I returned it to the right one, then moved on to several other boxes. It was hardly proper archaeology, but it was the best I could do.

After I'd filled my bag with four artifacts that contained nearly-decayed magic and taken the needed pictures, I stood.

"All done," I said.

"Good. Let's scram."

"Agreed." This was one of the most amazing pyramids I'd ever been inside, but I didn't particularly like it. Between the dampening charm not working and the demons with fire swords, I hadn't had a postcard-worthy experience here.

Though it was weird that more demons hadn't shown up this time around once I'd started fussing with the treasure. I didn't like that at all. Not one little bit.

Were they supposed to be guarding the treasure, or had my nullification powers made my concealment charm fail? Because if it was the latter...

The monster could find me. And the last person I wanted to run into was Victor Orriodor.

"Yeah, it's a dud." Nix turned the dampening cuff over in her hands, then looked at me, sorrow in her green eyes. "For you, at least. It's not strong enough."

"Damn." I leaned back on the couch and stared at the ceiling of my apartment, my chest feeling empty.

Del and I had made the slow journey back across the desert, returned the camels to their owners, and transported to our shop, Ancient Magic, where we'd dropped off the artifacts.

By the time we'd gotten back, it'd been after five. Nix, who normally watched the front counter, had been cooped up in the shop all day, so she'd insisted we get the hell out of there. She'd wanted to go to Potions & Pastille's, our friends' coffee shop/whiskey bar, but I'd insisted on a shower first.

I had sand everywhere. And demon blood. And sweat. Basically, I was a nightmare. If it were Halloween, I wouldn't need a costume.

And we had an evening memorial service to attend at seven, so showing up covered in blood was not a great idea.

While I'd showered, Nix had fished a Pabst Blue Ribbon—my hillbilly hipster beer of choice—out of the fridge and handed it to me through the curtain.

"You're a lifesaver," I'd said.

And she was, quite literally. Nix, Del, and I were sisters by choice. *Deirfiúr*, in our native Irish. We'd awoken in a field at fifteen with no memories except that we were FireSouls on the run from someone who wanted to hurt us. We'd called him the Monster, though we'd recently learned he was named Victor Orriodor. In the ten years we'd hidden from him, we'd saved each other countless times.

"So you're telling me it could work," I said. "Just that the nullification power I'm saddled with is too strong for the dampening charm to have much effect."

"Yep. There are a few dampening charms out there of different strengths. There's one at the Museum for Magical History that's super strong." She made an explosion motion with her hands.

"Yeah?" Hope flared in my chest.

"Too strong. As in, obliterate-all-your-magic strong. It's actually a pretty terrifying piece of magic. What you need is a Goldilocks dampener—just strong enough."

"Yeah." But I took the golden cuff back from her and slipped it on my wrist. She gave me a look, but I ignored it.

"It was a long shot anyway," Nix said. "Dampening the nullification enough to allow your normal powers to shine through wasn't all that likely to begin with."

"I know, but I'm desperate. Aethelred the Shade hasn't been seen in a week." Last week, the old seer had recognized a necklace I'd had since childhood and promised to tell me more, though there hadn't been time at that moment. "He was my only link to information about my past, and maybe getting my power back, but he's hiding out like a mole."

Nix reached over and gripped my hand. Her green gaze was intense as she said, "We'll find him. We have plenty of people looking, and Aidan is following up on a lead right now."

Aidan was my friend. Possibly my boyfriend also, if you could call a giant of a man who was the most powerful Shifter in the world something as juvenile as *boyfriend*. We'd spent almost two months together, trying to keep our heads above water as Victor Orriodor had thrown challenge after challenge at me.

"Yeah. I know. I'm determined to fix this. It's just that I'm not handling things well at all." In the past week, I'd spent more time mired in self-doubt and pity than I ever had in my life. I didn't like who I was becoming, and though I tried to fight it, I didn't think I was doing a great job.

Del's signature knock sounded at the door. *Rap-rap-rappity-rap.*

"Come in!" I yelled.

She entered, looking bright and clean. The blood and grime had been replaced with her usual black leather.

Black leather was her bounty hunting wear, but I think she also liked looking like a badass. With her black hair, blue eyes, and wicked sword, she was a top notch badass.

My usual attire of jeans, tall boots, t-shirt, and a fitted brown leather jacket wasn't nearly as cool as her stuff, but it worked for me.

"Want a beer?" I asked.

She eyed my can of PBR doubtfully. "Not that swill."

"Yeah, yeah, fancy pants. I put some of that jet fuel IPA you like in the fridge."

"You're too good to me. But it's not jet fuel, you heathen. It's high gravity."

"Snob."

"Then someone will have to drive to the memorial service," Del said. "Because I'm tapped out." Though Del could transport anywhere and bring two people with her, her power wasn't unlimited. She'd used it all up bringing us back from Egypt.

"Then it's your lucky day, because I'm driving." Nix held up her bottle of water to indicate she wasn't having a beer. "So you might as well have one."

"You convinced me."

I grinned as she walked toward my tiny kitchen. Though I lived on the top floor of the building we rented, most of it was reserved for my treasure trove, which was full of weapons and leather jackets and boots. Living quarters were teeny.

Del returned to the living room. "Any word on that dampening charm?"

"Won't work," I said, shifting my arm so she couldn't see that I wore the cuff. I knew it didn't work, but maybe…

"Don't worry. We'll find a way—"

"Thank you for your help, Del. We'll find a way to get my powers back. I know." Sympathy cued my water works, and I didn't want to hear it.

Did I though? I'd only been trying to get them back for a week, and it already felt a bit hopeless. But there was no way in hell I was giving up, so, hopeless or not, I'd be slogging through.

"I just want you to know you did a good thing, taking the Nullifier's power," Del said. "Whenever you're feeling down about losing your innate gifts, just keep in mind—you and he saved Magic's Bend. Hundreds of lives. Our town would have been sucked into that portal if it weren't for you and the Nullifier."

"Yeah," Nix said. "The Monster would've won."

He'd created the portal. To break the portal before it could consume the town, we'd asked a Nullifier to come help destroy it. But the Monster had killed him. I'd used my FireSoul ability to take the Nullifier's power and finish the job.

The memorial service tonight was for the Nullifier. He shouldn't have had to die to save Magic's Bend. But he had. And the local government and the Order of the Magica wanted to hold a ceremony to honor him.

I was all for that. Normally, I wouldn't have gone near an event that put me in the way of Order members. But with my new nullification power, my own FireSoul ability was stifled to the point that they shouldn't be able to sense that part of me. I should be nothing but a magical void.

After the ceremony, I was supposed to meet the Order of the Magica representatives to receive their thanks for my part in the whole thing. I didn't want that part, though Aidan was right—the Order would be hella suspicious if I didn't show. And I wanted to go to honor the Nullifier. Though I wasn't looking forward to it.

I had to hope my spotty nullification ability didn't fade out on me so that I could keep a low profile.

"Don't call him the Monster," I said. "We made up that name when we were young and afraid of him. He'd probably like it. So let's use his boring, miserable name. Victor Orriodor. "

"Because fear of a name increases fear of the thing itself," Nix said, quoting Dumbledore.

"Exactly." I nodded. If one couldn't go to Dumbledore for advice, where could one go?

"Harry Potter nuts." Del grinned.

Nix and I clinked our drinks together.

Del glanced at the clock. "We should get going. Don't want to be late. Are we meeting Aidan there?"

While Del and I had gone to the pyramid to find the dampening charm, Aidan had been working on his own lead, locating Aethelred's known associates and trying to find tracking charms. We'd borrowed three from Aethelred, and when we finally found him, we wanted to give him the replacements…otherwise he might not talk to us.

"Let's do it, then." I set down my half-drunk beer. "Let me grab my jacket."

"Can we take your car?" Nix asked. "Mine is leaking something weird."

"Think you can handle Cecelia?"

"For sure."

"Hmmm, questionable." Cecelia was the old junker I'd bought about five years ago when we'd finally earned enough money to escape our old boss—Old Man Bastard, OMB for short. Cecelia had been running fine ever since. A bit persnickety maybe, but fine.

I went to my room and grabbed a black leather jacket, different from my usual brown. But this was a memorial service. They wouldn't be getting me into a dress, but the least I could do was wear black.

I shrugged it on and took my daggers off the dresser, carefully strapping them into my thigh sheaths. It was a good thing Magic's Bend was an all-magic city, hidden from human eyes, or people would have looked at me strange. As it was, I blended well. Even at a memorial service, the weapons wouldn't stand out too much.

I joined Nix and Del, and we went single file down the narrow stairs, past Del's apartment on the third floor and Nix's on the second. Ancient Magic was on the bottom.

The sun was setting as we made our way out the green door and across the street to Cecelia. The old car sat in front of the park that was opposite Factory Row, where we lived and worked. Rent was low and the company was weird, which made it perfect as far as I was concerned.

And on late summer evenings like this, it was hard to believe there was a better place to live. Though the flattering light couldn't conceal Cecelia's chipped paint and dented bumpers, I loved the old girl and wouldn't get another car 'til she sputtered her last.

Not to mention, living on Factory Row and driving an old junker allowed me to put all my spare money toward padding my trove.

"Shotgun!" I called.

Del groaned and climbed into the backseat. Nix and I got in, and she cranked the ignition. She drove through town like a maniac, zipping by the tall buildings of the business district and the ornate, 18th century buildings in the historic part of town. We passed Darklane, where everyone knew the black magic practitioners lived, and I peered at Aethelred's window as we passed.

It was dark and empty.

Damn.

By the time we pulled into the parking lot at the Museum of Magical history, I was slightly queasy from Nix's Mario Kart driving.

"I really wish they hadn't chosen this place," I said as we climbed out of the car.

It'd been more than a week since the portal had sucked in half the museum and the big brick building looked entirely normal again, but I'd had enough of it for a while.

"I guess they wanted to prove that everything is okay now," Del said.

"And the Nullifier's sacrifice did save this place." Nix shoved the keys into her pocket.

I rubbed my chest absently as we set off across the parking lot toward the huge brick museum.

"You doing okay?" Nix asked.

"Yeah. Just a tic." I'd developed it after losing my powers. Like a person with a stomachache rubs their stomach, I rubbed my chest. I could feel the emptiness.

We climbed the massive stairs to the front of the museum. An imposing figure in a conservative black dress stood in front of the door. Her dark hair was scraped back from her forehead, and keen green eyes peered out from behind dark spectacles. The magic that radiated from her was strong and smelled like some kind of incense.

Her gaze snapped to me, and I realized where I'd seen her before.

An Order investigator. Her job was to fix problems and sniff out FireSouls. A cold sweat broke out on my skin, and I tried not to look shifty.

This was exactly the kind of person I didn't want to run into here. It was her job to find my kind and throw them in the Prison for Magical Miscreants. That fate had always been my greatest fear. Nix and Del had good control of their power, but I never had. They could be around Order members without igniting suspicion, but that idea was foreign to me. Even with the nullification masking my own magic, I was still trembling. The fear was too ingrained.

I nodded at her as we walked past to reach the door, trying to keep my breathing even. Her gaze followed me, burning into my back.

We passed through the large doors into the main lobby of the museum, which was set up with a temporary stage at the far end and rows of folding chairs in the middle. Subdued flower arrangements had been placed at either end of the stage, giving the whole thing a funeral-like feel.

Lilies. The worst funeral flower.

"This is going to be a blast," I said, then felt like a jerk. The whole point of this was to honor the Nullifier, who'd died to protect us all. I really needed to get my head out of my butt.

"Agreed," Del said.

A crowd milled in the middle of the huge room, far more people than I'd expected. Several hundred, at least. It'd be standing room only.

A moment later, Aidan appeared in the crowd. His gray gaze landed on me, and a smile stretched across his face.

I grinned and jerked my chin upward in that lame greeting that frat boys do. It was ridiculous, but then, *I* was a bit ridiculous when I was around Aidan.

I'd started off our acquaintance all cool and collected. The collected had gone out the window pretty quickly, and now I was just trying to play it cool.

I was probably failing.

Aidan strode toward me, his big form easily cutting a path through the crowd. He was well over six feet and built like a Greek god—I'd gotten a peek last week and confirmed my suspicions that he looked even better out of his shirt—but it was his face that was frankly ludicrous. People shouldn't be as handsome as he was. It made the rest of us uncomfortable. He looked like some kind of model—the rugged kind, not the pretty kind—and I wanted to point at myself and go "*me?*" every time he made it clear he liked me.

"Hey," he said as he neared.

"Hey yourself."

"Come here." He put a hand behind my waist and pulled me toward him, then brushed a kiss against my cheek as he murmured in my ear, "Missed you."

His rough voice sent a shiver over my skin. "Missed you, too. Did your lead work out?" I asked as Nix and Del joined my side.

"No. I can't find transport charms anywhere. I've had four people on it for the last week, me included. Every wizard they check is suddenly sold out. And we've done everything we can to convince them to sell to us, but it's not working."

So, massive amounts of money, then. Aidan was the Origin, a descendent of the first Shifter, and currently the most powerful one in the world. In addition to being a massive badass of that nature, he was also ridiculously wealthy. Over the last month, he'd thrown a bit of that money around in scenarios like this.

Scenarios meant to protect me.

"Something weird is going on," Nix said. "Transport charms have always been hard to come by, but not impossible."

"Maybe I need to start making some," Del said.

It was one of her gifts, related to her own ability to transport, but it was difficult to do and sapped her power for a long time, so we normally relied on buying them from wizards.

"Maybe," I said.

"It's Victor Orriodor, isn't it?" Nix asked. "He's responsible for the scarcity of the charms."

"That was my thought. He's got something planned, and if his appearances in your life are any indication, he's gaining power."

I scrubbed a hand over my face, suddenly weary. "I think you're right. He needs those charms to sic his demons on me. And to capture other FireSouls. I just wish I knew what his endgame was."

Aidan reached for my hand and squeezed. "We'll figure it out."

"Yeah." I lifted my head. "We have to."

He nodded approvingly. "Come on. I want to hear what they have to say."

"Sure, but let's stick to the back." I followed him through the crowd, glancing back over my shoulder to make sure Nix and Del followed. Nix, who was right behind me, put her hands over her chest and made thumping heart motions. Del was making kissy faces behind Nix.

I hissed at them, then turned back around.

Aidan led us toward a darkened corner in the back where a massive statue of a female warrior loomed. It was perfect. She'd guard us, figuratively speaking, and I didn't like the idea of being surrounded by other Magica while my powers were gone.

I looked toward the crowd, and Dr. Garriso caught my eye. He made his way toward us, looking so much better than he had after I'd saved him from Victor Orriodor's portal last week. His white hair was neatly combed and his tweed suit freshly pressed. My shoulders loosened a bit. Thank magic he was okay. He was a tough old goat, and I was glad to see him back to his usual spry self.

But when he approached, the worry in his gaze was stark.

"Hi, Dr. Garriso. What's wrong?"

"We have done an inventory of the museum and found a missing item. A massive dampening charm encased in the Gundestrop cauldron. It's Celtic, and the artifact itself is ancient, found in a bog in Denmark. It's quite large and heavily decorated. But the dampening charm that it houses is even more impressive. It's the strongest of its kind, able to knock out the magical power of dozens of supernaturals at once."

My breath whooshed out. When I could breathe again, all I could do was wheeze, "Shit."

"And you have no idea what he might do with it?" Aidan asked.

"No, but I wanted to let you know. However he bypassed the museum's security, he put a lot of money and power into it."

That was no surprise. Victor Orriodor had a lot of both. But we were both seeking dampening charms? Why?

"Thank you for telling us, Dr. Garriso," I said. "I'm glad to see you are feeling better."

"Because of you, my dear."

I gave him a quick hug, and he left to find his seat.

"Well, that's a real kick in the pants," I muttered.

"No kidding." Del thumped her head back against the wall.

The lights flickered, signaling that the ceremony would begin soon.

"So how's this going to go?" I asked.

"It won't take long," Aidan said. "Just some speeches, then we'll meet the Order after. They'll thank you, and it'll be over."

Okay, that wasn't so bad. I just had to keep everything under control and act like a normal Magica.

I almost laughed. I'd never been normal, so this wouldn't be easy.

We stood in silence and watched the chairs fill up. The lights dimmed until our corner was cast entirely in shadow and a subtle yellow glow illuminated the stage and the depressing flowers. Freaking lilies. Magic's Bend might be full of Magica and Shifters, but our memorial practices were as dreary and boring as the humans'.

The museum looked so different tonight, full of people and not half disappearing from Victor Orriodor's portal.

But what was that bastard's end goal? When he'd created the portal, he'd done it to steal something from this museum. He'd managed to get his hands on the dampening charm, but also the Chalice of Youth, which had been in Dr. Garriso's office. Only a truly evil person could drink from it, and if they did, they'd become immortal.

So, definitely not a good thing to leave in the hands of a psychopath. But what he wanted with the dampening charm, I had no idea.

The lights on the stage glowed bright, catching my attention. A procession of black-clad Magica entered from the right. The power that rolled off them, varying signatures of all varieties, told me that they had to be upper-level members of the Order. They all strode out with slow steps, lending a gravity to their entrance that I was sure they got off on.

The last man to enter the stage came a few steps behind the rest. He wore an immaculate dark blue suit instead of black like the rest, but it was his face that made my skin turn cold.

Victor Orriodor.

He'd controlled his magic signature—the smell of rot and decay, the taste of death, and the feel of bee stings—so it seemed that the crowd had no idea what was in their midst.

My hand tightened on Aidan's as my heart threatened to break my ribs. Why the hell was he here? Was he an Order member?

I wasn't about to stick around to find out. Not when I didn't have my magic to protect me. He was outnumbered against all the Magica in the room, but there was no way I'd hang out and let him see me.

But the Celtic cauldron. If he had it here, he could dampen everyone's powers and overtake them.

I glanced at Del and Nix, whose wide eyes met my own.

"See if you can find the cauldron with your dragon sense. If it's in the building, we need to know."

They both closed their eyes, though their magic didn't give off much of a signature. They were both being careful to control it around this many Order members.

Nix opened her eyes first. "It's not here."

"Seconded," Del said.

Without the cauldron, he was definitely outnumbered. Whatever his reason for being here—and it might be because he was an Order member, magic forbid—he was playing the long game.

We had to get out of here. Nix jerked her head toward a side exit and I nodded, then tugged on Aidan's hand. His gaze snapped to mine and he nodded.

Heart racing, I followed Nix and Del, sticking to the shadows and trying not to jostle anyone. Aidan stuck close behind, his steps silent as we snuck out of the museum.

Near the exit, I caught sight of the familiar red fire alarm. I waved Nix, Del, and Aidan out, then pulled the lever. I hated to interrupt the Nullifier's memorial, but I wanted to interrupt Victor Orriodor's plans, whatever they were.

The siren blared as I ran out the door and met my friends' startled gazes.

"Good idea!" Nix said.

We took off, sprinting across the grass toward the parking lot. I'd snuck out like a coward.

But what was I going to do? Fight him with my questionable nullifying power? I'd practiced it but didn't have any kind of reliable skill with it. I'd be putting hundreds of people at risk.

We'd reached Cecelia and Aidan's car, which were conveniently parked next to each other, when my phone buzzed. I was so wired that I jumped and nearly screeched before I got it together enough to fumble my phone out of my pocket and look at the screen.

I read the name aloud. "Aerdeca."

"What does she want?" Del asked.

"Don't know." I hadn't spoken to the Blood Sorceress since last week, during the wayward portal disaster. But she'd been the one to recommend I go see Aethelred about finding a Nullifier to help destroy the portal. She knew I was looking for him now.

Maybe she'd found him!

I glanced around. We were hidden by the parked cars, and we had a minute before people arrived. More than likely, they'd stand in the museum's yard and wait to see if the museum lit up like a bonfire.

I clicked the answer button. "Hello?"

"Cass?" Aerdeca's clear voice filled my ear. "Meet me at the Assassin's Brew. Darklane. Now."

The line clicked.

I stared down at the phone. "Looks like we're going to Darklane. I think Aerdeca and Mordaca have something to tell us."

"You trust her?"

I shrugged. "Enough to go. They might have the info we need."

CHAPTER THREE

Aidan and I followed Del and Nix to Darklane. By the time we pulled into the creepy neighborhood, I was nearly vibrating with nerves, hoping that Aerdeca and Mordaca would tell me where Aethelred had gone.

Aerdeca and her sister, Mordaca, ran the Apothecary's Jungle, a shop in Darklane that specialized in Blood Sorcery, Aerdeca and Mordaca's particular gifts. I'd gone to them for help once, but it'd been pricey. If they had info now, I wondered how much it would cost.

Dark figures lurked in shadows, watching our car as it drove slowly by. Buildings loomed on either side of the street, cutting out the last of the setting sun. Though they were only three stories high, they always seemed to block out the light. Even at high noon. Their historic fronts were covered with grime, lending the place its name.

Darklane was where you lived if you worked with magic's darker side. The kind that harmed as well as helped. But that didn't necessarily make it bad. It was all up to interpretation.

Though these supernaturals were occasionally on the wrong side of the law, most weren't outright lawbreakers. The Magica didn't tolerate that. Folks in Darklane walked the line with things like blood magic—illegal if done without the consent of the donor, but otherwise acceptable.

Aidan slowed the car to a crawl, and we rolled by the narrow buildings, looking for the sign for Assassin's Brew. I'd never been to that bar because I liked to stay out of Darklane. Just because most people here weren't outright criminals didn't mean there wasn't a higher percentage of them. Though it wasn't the criminals I was worried about. It was the cops. More criminals equaled more cops, and I wasn't about to hang out in a place where the Order of the Magica was more likely to be looking for wrongdoing.

My existence as a FireSoul meant that I was pretty much always guilty. No way in hell I was increasing my chances of getting tossed in the Prison for Magical Miscreants.

"There it is." I pointed to a building that had once been blue. A sign hung over the door that read Assassin's Brew. The letter A was formed with two daggers. Clever.

Aidan found a parking spot along the street, and we climbed out of the car. Ornate, Oliver Twistian street lamps shined yellow light on the grimy sidewalk.

I dodged a suspicious blue goo that stuck to the ground and met Nix and Del by the door. I couldn't say my fingers didn't twitch toward my knives even though I knew Darklane was mostly safe.

But in the magical world, you couldn't take *mostly* to the bank. Without my magic, I felt a bit naked. I reminded myself that I'd spent most of my life relying on my wits and weapons, so I'd be fine now.

The windows on either side of the door glowed warmly. Inside, people crowded around the bar and hunched over small tables. I pulled open the heavy wooden door and slipped inside, Del, Nix, and Aidan at my back.

Voices were muted, and the ceiling was low. It was a real old-school pub with lots of wood and only a few taps. There were no blue liqueurs behind the bar, unless you counted the weird potions for sale. But nothing called Wicked or Sexxxy, like you'd find at a city club.

Aerdeca and Mordaca sat on bar stools near the wall, looking entirely too fabulous to be in a place like this. As usual, Mordaca looked like Elvira, with her plunging, slinky black dress, bouffant black hair, and mask-like eye makeup. Aerdeca was her golden opposite, wearing an elegant white pantsuit that she magically managed to pull off. I was beginning to wonder if that was her uniform in the same way that Elvira-chic was Mordaca's.

They both waved at us, an identical flutter of their fingertips. Mordaca's nails were black points, Aerdeca's white.

"Those chicks have their shit together," Del muttered as she eyed their outfits.

"Yep." We were a different breed, that was for sure. But I still liked Mordaca and Aerdeca.

Yeah, they were a bit scary, but I respected that.

Aerdeca smiled serenely as we approached. Mordaca's red lips remained straight and her gaze impassive.

"Cass. How're you?" Aerdeca's gaze was sharp. And curious.

We hadn't told anyone what had happened to my magic, but she could probably sense my altered power signature and wondered about it.

"I'm great. You?"

"I'm well," Aerdeca said.

I met Mordaca's gaze. "You?"

"Fabulous." But Mordaca's dark gaze was haunted.

When the portal had frozen the museum, she'd been trapped inside. I got the impression she'd been conscious the whole time. Being trapped like that for days would give anyone nightmares. No wonder they hadn't been at the memorial, even though the Nullifier's sacrifice had saved Mordaca.

"You're looking for Aethelred." Mordaca raised her smoking gray cocktail to her lips and sipped.

She'd stated the obvious. We'd asked them to keep an eye out for him since they knew him, but Mordaca probably wanted me on edge, explaining myself.

"Yes. Aerdeca helped us before."

Aerdeca sipped her clear martini—straight vodka served in a fancy glass with a couple olives, if I had to guess—and said, "No. I helped *us*." She indicated herself and her sister. "You needed Aethelred to find the Nullifier, which in turn saved my sister."

When Mordaca had been trapped by the expanding portal, Aerdeca had spat out Aethelred's location real quick. Now that her sister was no longer in danger, I had a feeling she was about to be a lot more close-lipped.

"Right," I said. "Which I did. And because I stopped the portal—and saved Mordaca, don't forget—I now need Aethelred's help. He knows things I need to know."

"Well, he's hiding for a reason," Mordaca said, her raspy voice sounding like she smoked three packs a day. "Otherwise, he'd be back in town. Tuesdays are Black Bingo night, and he hasn't missed one of those in a decade. So whatever has him staying away is serious."

What the hell was Black Bingo? Probably something creepy, considering that this was Darklane. I wouldn't ask.

"And you were the last person he saw before he left town last week," Aerdeca said. "So, perhaps you're the one he is hiding from."

"All we did last week was talk," I said. "About how to find the Nullifier to stop the portal. He said he'd answer my questions if I stopped the portal. I did that. Now I just want to see him."

"Well, I'm not certain that your friend here can pay the right price." Aerdeca ran her gaze over Aidan. She might look like the nicer one, with her white outfits and sweeter voice, but she was the scarier one in this pair.

Aidan turned to loom over them. "Oh, I'm certain I can. If not in money, then in threats."

If I hadn't known Aidan so well, the ice in his deep voice would have sent shivers across my skin.

Aerdeca's gaze widened only a fraction, but it was enough to tell that she understood. And probably liked the scary side of Aidan.

"You have a lovely shop," Aidan said. "Which I'm sure is entirely up to code."

Meaning that it didn't break any of the Order of the Magica's dark magic laws.

Aerdeca's brows lowered. "Of course it is."

"Of course. Which means that a visit from my friend at the Order's Magic Enforcement Division would be most welcome."

Her knuckles whitened where she gripped the bar. "Absolutely. Or, you could pay us five grand and we'll give you what you want."

A smile tugged at the corner of Aidan's mouth. "That sounds fair."

"That sounds expensive," I said.

"I imagine the answers you seek are worth far more to you," Mordaca said. "Your magic smells...different."

I snapped my mouth shut.

She was right.

The answers were worth my life. Five grand was measly compared to that. And technically, I had the money from a big job I'd done a few weeks ago.

"Fine. But I'll pay it," I said.

"Cash now," Mordaca said.

I scowled. No way I carried that kind of money around.

Aidan pulled out his wallet. Of course he carried around that much cash. It wasn't like anyone was going to mug the Origin.

He handed over a crisp stack of bills.

"Thanks," I said to him. "I'll pay you back."

He glanced over, his expression making it clear how stupid he thought that idea was.

I scowled.

He totally wasn't going to take the money. But Aerdeca opened her mouth to speak, and I pushed the concern away. I could deal with Aidan later.

"Aethelred is at his summer home, apparently," Mordaca said.

"But he's our friend," Aerdeca said. "We'll sell you a chance to talk to him, but we won't sell *him*. We'll blindfold you and take you to him. If he wants to see you, he will. And if you hurt him, you're dead."

"Dead in a really miserable manner." Mordaca tapped her black claws on the bar, the threat clear.

"I don't want to hurt him."

"Well, he's hiding for a reason."

"Where is his summer home?" The back of my neck itched. Fiercely. That *someone-is-watching* feeling, but far worse. I shivered and glanced around, but saw no one. I turned back to Mordaca and Aerdeca, not wanting to miss a word.

But I couldn't get over the feeling of someone watching.

"He lives in a tree?" I gazed at the enormous oak. Aerdeca had just removed my blindfold. A door and windows were carved into the trunk. Light glowed from the tiny window in the door. The branches and leaves above were green and vibrant. "Like those elves who make cookies?"

"I don't make cookies!" a crotchety voice yelled from within. "And certainly not for you!"

"Moody," I murmured to Aidan, who stood at my side.

Mordaca poked me in the back.

I scowled at her. But despite my joke, my heart raced. This was the man who had answers about my past. And who'd been hiding from me for some reason.

Aerdeca and Mordaca had been true to their word, blindfolding us and piling us into their little sports car, then driving about two hours. There hadn't been enough space in Aerdeca's tiny car, so Nix and Del had stayed behind.

From the size of these massive trees, we were in one of the woodland areas surrounding Magic's Bend. Maybe near the coast. Glittering lights in the trees around us indicated pixies. We were in Wistman's Wood, maybe, which was an old forest near the Oregon coast. It was haunted with pixies, hence its name, a derivative of Whistman, meaning one who has been pixie-led. We hadn't seen any pixies so far, though, so maybe we were in one of the less well-known enchanted forests in Oregon.

"Can we come in, Aethelred?" I called.

He sighed so loudly that I could hear it through the door. "All right."

The heavy wooden door creaked open slowly. Warm air gusted out, along with the very distinct smell of chocolate chip cookies.

My mouth watered.

"Really?" I asked the old man, whose long white beard reached nearly to his waist. "You don't make cookies?"

"Sheer coincidence." He huffed and adjusted his blue velour track suit.

Once again, he looked like Gandalf on his way to senior aerobics. This outfit was a slightly darker shade of blue than it had been last time, but I was noticing a theme.

He looked at Aerdeca and Mordaca, who stood to my left. "Will you come in?"

"No," Mordaca said. "We've a colleague to see who lives on the other side of the hollow."

Aerdeca looked at me. "Call us when you are done. We will come get you. We'll see you later, Aethelred."

"Yes. At Black Bingo." He scowled at us.

He was huffier than he had been the last time we'd come to him for help. "I'm sorry about the Nullifier."

The Nullifier had been his friend. Because I'd roped him into helping us save Magic's Bend, he was dead. I wouldn't blame Aethelred if he was angry with me. *I* was angry with me. I could have done a lot of things differently and maybe saved his life.

"Yes. So am I." His blue gaze darkened. "I try to take heart in the fact that he chose his path willingly. And he'd lived a long time."

Centuries, in fact. The Nullifier's power also nullified death. Something it was doing for me, but I certainly didn't want it. To watch my family and friends die around me? No thanks.

Trauma could kill me, like it had the Nullifier, but I didn't want to die in battle or take my own life. I wanted to die an old lady, surrounded by a dozen fat cats wearing sweaters I'd crocheted for them.

"True, he did live a long time," I said.

"But the bastard who killed him still lives?"

"Victor Orriodor, yes." The Monster. No matter how many times I used his real name, I couldn't help but think of him that way. "But I'll find him eventually. And kill him."

Aethelred's sharp gaze zeroed in on Aidan. "And you? Have you come to return my transport charms?"

Aidan and I had borrowed three rare transport charms from Aethelred last week. We'd needed them to help us travel quickly enough to defeat the portal.

"Unfortunately, no," Aidan said. "They've become even more scarce recently. I have men looking for them, going to each wizard who creates them, but they've all been sold to an unknown buyer. But I guarantee I will replace the ones we borrowed as soon as my men find some."

"I do hope so." He stepped back and gestured us in. "You might as well come in and get this over with."

He seemed to be in a rush. "Why the hurry? And why haven't you returned to Magic's Bend?"

"You're dangerous." He turned and walked into the room. "It's better for my life expectancy if I'm not around you."

"Dangerous?" I followed him.

The inside of the tree was warm and inviting, all golden wood tones and colorful fabric on the furniture.

The space was round, which was fitting for a tree, with a small sitting area, a kitchen, a little table, and a spiral staircase leading up to a loft. Books cluttered the shelves, but it wasn't nearly as chaotic as Aethelred's place in Darklane.

"What do you mean, I'm dangerous?" I asked as Aidan and I took the couch he gestured toward. It sat near a small electric fireplace. Smart, considering we were in a tree. "Not to you."

"No, but those who hunt you are dangerous." He dropped heavily into the chair across from us.

"They can't find me. I have a concealment charm."

"Do you?" His sharp blue gaze met mine.

"What do you mean?"

"Have you felt odd lately? As if someone were watching you?"

The hair on my arms stood up. "How did you know?"

"Ever since you came to see me over a week ago, I've kept my inner eye on watch for you. I think your concealment charm may be failing. Enemies are circling you. And you don't have long until you meet."

"What?" My breath felt scarce.

"I can't see it clearly. But a confrontation is coming. Someone seeks you to do harm. Their seer will find you soon enough, and then they will come."

"They may already have." The demons in the pyramid. Maybe they hadn't been guards, but rather scouts sent by Victor when his seer caught sight of me. "Earlier today, some demons appeared. We killed them, but they haven't come for me since."

"As long as you possess the Nullifier's power, your concealment charm will fail. As his power battles with your own, your concealment charm will go in and out. Perhaps the seer saw you for a moment and sent the demons. Now, he cannot see you."

"But he could again." Worry creased Aidan's brow.

"He could. As long as you have the Nullifier's power, you are at risk."

"But why? I've learned how to control other new powers." Lightning and illusion were my two favorites. "Why not the Nullifier's power?"

"It is unnatural to try to mesh power with anti-power, which is essentially what the Nullifier's gift is. They are canceling each other. Fighting for supremacy. And with you, it is worse. There is something about your power that is strange. Something that conflicts even more than normal with the Nullifier's anti-power. And you're fighting your new power, not embracing it as you should be."

Of course I was fighting it. It sucked. I fiddled with the golden cuff hidden under my jacket sleeve. "Can I get rid of the Nullifier's power and have my own back?"

His expression turned sad. "I have never heard of it happening."

Aidan reached for my hand. His voice was firm when he said, "There are many things that haven't happened that are still possible. Cass will get her power back."

"Maybe." The Nullifier held out his hand, as if to take mine. "May I?"

I pulled my palm from Aidan's warm grip and reached for Aethelred. A tingle of energy went up my arm when he gripped my hand. His magic tasted like cinnamon.

"Yes." Aethelred's gaze turned thoughtful. "As I thought. Your power is rare. There is more here than you realize. Not just lightning and illusion."

"My root power." Or did he mean my FireSoul?

"Perhaps."

"It was taken from me."

"Taken? Perhaps. Whatever it is, it is important. Powerful."

"Can I get it back?"

Aethelred let go of my hand, and his gaze cleared. "I cannot see that."

"Why not?" I knew why, but I was so desperate I blurted it anyway.

"Seers cannot perform on command." Indignation colored his voice. "Not only is it impossible, I would refuse."

I lowered my gaze. "I understand. I'm sorry. It's just that I *really* want my power back." I reached for the locket's clasp at the back of my neck and removed the small golden heart. "Before, you said you recognized my locket. And I had a dream about my past where I could feel my locket protecting me."

Aethelred reached for the gold necklace and took it. He studied it, his brows drawn over his eyes in concentration.

"Yes," he murmured. "It is important to your past."

"How so?"

"But you've never opened it." His gaze was focused on the locket, his voice distant.

"How can you tell?"

"It's a Metis locket, and the writing hasn't been disturbed." He held it up and indicated the delicate swirls impressed into the gold. "See?"

"I thought that was just decoration."

"No. It's the language of the Metis. Only one of their order can read the writing and unlock it."

I'd never heard of the Metis. "Where do I find them?"

"Greece. They're a small group of magical scholars who live on an island in the Aegean."

No wonder I'd never heard of them. I'd never been to Greece.

I looked at Aidan. "Then we'll go find them."

He nodded.

"They should be able to help you understand the locket," Aethelred said. "I cannot see how it is important to your past, but it is."

"Thank you."

"On your journey, you must be careful," he said. "Your enemies could find you at any time. Stay in protected places. And try to get your power back soon, if you can. I see a meeting between you and the one who killed the Nullifier."

Victor Orriodor. "When?"

"Within the week. You must have your power by then, or you will not survive. Even then, there are no guarantees."

CHAPTER FOUR

"We're about to land."

Aidan's words filtered into my sleep-logged mind. I jerked, then scrubbed my eyes and sat up, looking around. The small room was beautifully decorated in neutrals.

Right. I was in the bedroom of Aidan's private plane. We'd departed Aethelred's and driven back to Magic's Bend. On the way, I'd asked Aerdeca and Mordaca if they'd ever heard of an Order member named Victor Orriodor. They'd said they hadn't, but had offered to do some snooping for the right price.

Aidan had paid it while I'd vowed to pay him back—and pinched him when he'd just ignored me.

Aerdeca and Mordaca had dropped us off at the airport at Magic's Bend, where we'd boarded Aidan's private jet to go to Greece to find the Metis. Del was still regenerating her power from our trip to Egypt and we had no transport charms, so this was the fastest way.

"Did I pass out right away?" I asked. I hadn't slept since before the pyramid.

"Pretty much," Aidan said. "Fell asleep in your seat during takeoff, so I moved you here."

I vaguely remembered waking in the night, the rumble of the plane all around. I'd snuggled into Aidan, thinking that this was the best moment of my day.

And it had been.

"Come here," I said.

He grinned, his mouth tugging up at the corner in a half-smile that made my skin heat. He stepped toward me, so tall that his head nearly brushed the ceiling. I gestured for him to bend down. He obliged, his shoulders nearly blocking out the light. I grabbed his shirt to pull him close and kissed him, pressing my mouth to his.

His lips were warm and soft, and damn, did he know how to kiss. I sank into the kiss, wanting to stay there forever.

My stomach grumbled.

Aidan pulled away and laughed. "Come on, let's get you fed. Wheels will be touching down any minute, and you need your strength."

"Yeah, yeah, okay. But I'm taking a raincheck on that kiss." We'd never had a chance to take it all the way—and to be honest, I hadn't been ready. This was too real. Too important. I didn't want to screw it all up by, well…screwing. Better to wait 'til the right moment.

Aidan left the little bedroom, and I scrambled around for my bag. Nix had met us at the airport with a bag before we'd left. She and Del were staying behind to poke around to see if they could figure out what Victor Orriodor had been doing on that stage. If I needed their help, Del would teleport them to us immediately.

After pulling on my uniform of jeans, t-shirt, leather boots, and fitted leather jacket, I strapped my daggers to my thighs. Thank magic I had Lefty and Righty.

I made my way out to the cockpit as the pilot gave the announcement to find our seats. Aidan was carrying a coffee cup and muffin. He held them out, and I gratefully took both.

"Thanks."

"Anytime."

I found a big seat near a window, and Aidan sat next to me, reaching for my hand as I stared out of the plane. It was still dark, though near dawn. Somewhere in that black sea were a scatter of islands, and answers existed on one of them. Answers about my past. My parents. Hopefully, my future.

Answers that I hoped would save my life.

Waves crashed against the bow of our small boat as we rowed toward the white sand beach snuggled into a small cove. Cliffs rose on either side of the cove, and the sea around us glittered blue and clear in the dawn light.

Aidan rowed while I kept lookout. We'd landed on the closest island with an airstrip and gotten a boat to make the final journey to the island where the Metis lived. Fortunately, it wasn't far.

"When this is all done and life's back to normal, we should come back here," I said. "For vacation."

Surprise glinted in Aidan's eyes as he grinned. "You? Take a few days off of work?"

"Hey!" I punched him in the shoulder. "I take time off. But lately, I've had a lot on my plate."

Like Victor Orriodor hunting me. Losing my powers. My *deirfiúr* at risk. Possibly dying.

It'd been a busy month.

"You'll handle it." The confidence in his voice was exactly what I needed to hear. No "it'll be okay" or "I'll save you." Just confidence in my abilities. And he'd have my back if I needed it.

"I will." I nodded toward the cove beach, which was only a few yards away now. "We're almost there."

Aidan turned around and nodded, then slowed his strokes. We beached on the pale sand, and Aidan stashed the oars, then jumped out at the bow and pulled the boat onto the little beach.

"Thanks." I hopped out, keeping my beloved boots out of the seawater. I'd get them messy when I had to, but little things like this, I appreciated. I might have a few dozen more pairs stashed in my trove, but I still loved these.

The beach was only about twenty yards long with small cliffs rising thirty feet above our heads. The cliffs dipped down in the middle of the beach, providing a rough path onto the island.

"Ready?" I asked as I approached Aidan.

He grimaced briefly, his brow scrunching in the universal sign of discomfort.

"What's wrong?" Panic made my heart race. Aidan was impenetrable, as far as I'd seen. Was he ill?

"Your nullifying power," he said. "You lost control of it for a moment."

"Shit, I'm sorry." The memory of what it'd felt like to have the Nullifier squash my power was not a good one. It was all around awful. "I felt like I had it under control. It just happened."

"I know."

"But that's the scary part," I said. "If I can't even control the Nullifier's power, then I'm a walking threat to myself and everyone around me."

He reached for my hand and tugged me toward the path. "Let's go. We'll find answers with the Metis."

We hurried up the dry path, dust kicking up beneath our feet. Scrubby brushes dotted the dry hills on either side of us. When we reached the top, a massive white temple complex loomed on the hill ahead. White pillars rose high into the bright blue sky. It was all very ancient Greece.

We were only fifty yards away when there was a crackle of magic in the air. Instinctually, my hands went for the daggers at my thighs.

"Incoming," Aidan said.

A moment later, over a dozen demons appeared, their hulking forms dotting the dry landscape around us. Shadow demons—gray ones with horns that arced back along their skulls—and the fire sword demons from the pyramid. I didn't know what those were called, but shadow demons had worked for Victor Orriodor in the past. I'd bet my trove they worked for him now.

71

Aidan's magic filled the air, bringing with it the scent of the forest and the sound of crashing waves. Light shimmered around him, and a moment later, a massive golden griffin stood in his place. Talons as long as daggers extended from each foot, and his beak was big enough to carry cows.

"Don't fly!" I yelled.

Normally, Aidan would take to the sky with his enormous wings, wiping out dozens of demons in quick succession. But with my nullifying power on the fritz, I could zap his power, and he could plummet to his death.

He nodded his massive head, his golden gaze on me, and sprinted for the fire sword demons nearest us. His footsteps thundered, vibrating the ground. He nimbly dodged their burning blades as he leapt at them and bit off their heads with his enormous beak. Blood sprayed and I gagged, looking away to find my own demons.

I drew my daggers and flung Righty at the smoke demon who was about to blast me with a burning jet. The shining black blade sunk into his chest and he toppled, his face twisted with pain. Before he could hit the ground, I nicked my finger with Lefty, calling Righty back to me.

I caught the blade as two shadow demons hurled their burning jets of smoke at me. I dodged one, but was hit by another. Hot smoke blasted into me and threw me backward. I slammed into the ground, pain radiating through my back.

This was such bullshit.

I scrambled to my feet, desperately wanting to control my nullifying power. But there was no way I could dampen our enemies' power without also dampening Aidan's. He was safer and stronger in his griffin form. And I was just as likely to only dampen him, leaving him vulnerable.

So daggers it was.

I spun to face the oncoming demons. Three shadow demons had raised their hands to throw their ammo, and two fire sword demons came at me from either side. Aidan was occupied with five of his own demons.

With just my daggers, these odds were looking bad.

I raised Righty and flung it at the closest fire sword demon. The blade pierced his neck, and I called it back immediately. I caught the flying dagger as three blasts of smoke flew at me. I dodged all but one, which hit me in the leg and knocked me over.

Pain blazed up my leg from the heat. Over the top of my high boot, my jeans were singed and burned, the skin beneath slightly fried.

A flash of white caught my eye as I staggered to my feet. Five white robed figures raced down the temple steps.

Backup.

At least, I hoped so.

They threw jets of light at the demons, blasting them backward.

"Hurry!" one of the women yelled. Her dark hair blew in the wind. "Get inside!"

I raced toward her, limping on my bad leg, my lungs burning. Aidan joined me. When I narrowly dodged a blast of smoke, Aidan raced ahead and dropped to a knee so that his back was low to the ground. I scrambled onto him, and he raised his wings on either side, creating a protective wall around me, then sprinted toward the temple steps.

I crouched low and clung to him as he thundered up the stairs. The white-robed figures continued to throw their blasts of light, knocking the demons back.

"This way!" The dark-haired woman gestured for us to enter the temple through the great white gate. Carved marble figures peered down at us from all sides. They were all draped in robes as well. "It is safe inside."

Aidan crossed under the gate, entering a symmetrical courtyard surrounded on all sides by columns and white marble buildings. In the middle, a fountain spewed clear, glittering water into a large square pool.

Steps led up to the many buildings and walkways. It was all Classical architecture done in marble, like the ancient ruins of Greece, but preserved perfectly.

Trees grew in patches, shielding marble benches. Scholars sat in the shade, writing in notebooks. At least, I thought they were scholars. They certainly looked serious enough with their furrowed brows, some wearing togas and some wearing tweed suits.

I slid off Aidan's back, and a shimmer of gray light surrounded him as he transformed back into a man. Once he was human again, his concerned gaze darted to my leg. He frowned, then approached, wrapping an arm around my waist. I leaned into him gratefully, taking some of the weight off the bad limb.

"How's the leg?" he asked.

"I've had worse." Though it hurt like a demon bite.

Aidan leaned over and hovered his hand over my calf. Cooling relief radiated from his palm as he used his healing gift to mend the worst of my injury. It still smarted, but it was vastly better.

"That's the extent of what I can do," he said and stood. "But if it still bothers you, they should have a healer here."

I put weight on the leg and it only hurt a bit, so I shook my head. "I'm fine. Thank you for that."

The woman who had gestured us into the compound approached. She had bright gray eyes and a serene expression.

"Thank you for saving us," I said.

"Not at all, Cassiopeia Clereaux and Aidan Merrick. Welcome to the Lyceum of Metis."

Aidan nodded his thanks while I racked my memory for my knowledge of Ancient Greece. Lyceum meant a school of some kind, which meant that Metis probably referred to the Titaness by that name. Metis was also known as the Mother of Wisdom, if I was remembering right.

But what was more interesting was that this woman knew my whole name, which had been chosen by my fifteen-year-old self when I'd woken in a field with no memories.

"You're a seer," I said.

"Indeed. Ophelia Dominiki. I woke this morning with the knowledge that you would be visiting." She glanced back at the gate and the other Lyceum guardians who were returning from the short battle. "Though I did not realize you would bring…friends."

The corner of my mouth tugged upward. "They're hardly friends. And I didn't realize I'd be bringing them either."

"I suppose I did get that impression," she said. "Would you like to come with me? I believe you have questions for us."

"Yes," I said.

We followed her through the courtyard and up the steps of one of the larger buildings.

"How long has this place been here?" I asked.

"Over six thousand years," she said. "At that time, Greece was the natural place for an institution of knowledge and learning."

She nodded her head toward an older man sitting on a bench against the wall, his gaze absorbed in a book. His form was slightly faded and gray, as if he were from an old photograph. "That's Cicero."

My brows rose appreciatively. That was pretty cool. "So, this is like an afterlife for smart people?"

"A bit. We are an institution of knowledge and learning. We are strongest when we have the best scholars. At death, they are offered an opportunity to come here. Some do and we are fortunate for it."

I liked Ophelia. She was calm and straightforward, and though I couldn't read auras, I had a feeling hers would be good.

"This way." She led us into a cool, brightly-lit room. Wide windows cast gleaming sunlight over the marble. We walked through elegantly decorated halls and rooms until we reached a space that was simpler, yet grander than any I'd ever seen.

The ceiling soared high above, covered in intricate marble carvings. They were geometric, all angles and straight lines, and they were riveting. Benches with cushions scattered the place, along with low tables set with wine and fruit. Bookshelves soared high against the walls, their contents neatly organized.

Individuals dressed in white robes reclined on benches, reading or eating. There were about a dozen of them, varying in age and race. Heads turned toward us as we entered. Ophelia nodded and they rose, then seated themselves at an area in the middle where eight marble benches were positioned in a circle.

A small pool sat in the middle, the water glittering blue. There was something riveting about it, a shimmer of magic or light that I couldn't identify.

"Come." Ophelia led us to one of the benches.

We sat, Ophelia and Aidan on either side of me.

"Cassiopeia Clereaux and Aidan Merrick have arrived. They have questions."

The ten robed figures who surrounded us nodded gravely.

I unclasped the locket and held it out. "I was told that you could read the writing on the back of this locket."

Ophelia took it and studied it, then passed it around. "We can do more than read it. We helped create it. The engraving on the back is our language."

The charm made its way around the room, passed from scholar to scholar.

A beautiful, dark-skinned woman looked at the charm, then met my gaze. "I am Nuria, and I enchanted this locket."

My heart thundered in my ears. This woman might know about my past.

"Cassiopeia is your real first name," she said.

"You mean, the one given by my parents?"

"Yes. You may have chosen it when you had no memory, but you were drawn to it specifically. Clereaux is your chosen last name, but the one you were gifted at birth was McFane. You are the daughter of Alice and Ethan McFane."

A dull noise roared in my head. "You knew my parents."

"Indeed." Her dark gaze met mine. "They were members of an organization that allies with ours."

"Were," I said. Past tense. My heart plummeted, a sick feeling filling my stomach. This emptiness was nothing compared to the Nullifier's magic.

Aidan reached for my hand. I squeezed it hard. I hadn't really expected my parents to still be alive, but I hadn't been able to control my hope.

Her gaze softened. "Yes, *were*. I am sorry."

"How?"

"That is not my story to tell," she said.

"Then whose is it? I want to know what happened to my parents." I gripped Aidan's hand harder, trying to control the tone of my voice. I was so close to answers! So close to a person who could tell me.

"They have closer friends than I who should share that story."

"Who? Were they part of the organization you spoke of?"

"Yes, but we do not speak their name, for they do not exist. Not on this side. And they will not exist if the Order of the Magica discovers them."

"Can you tell me how to find them?"

"Unfortunately, no. They are well hidden for safety."

Who the hell had my parents been involved with?

"You operate outside of the Order's jurisdiction?" Aidan asked, curiosity in his voice.

"We operate according to our own codes and laws," Ophelia said. "When the Order requests our help, we lend it. But we will not be governed by politicians. Knowledge often defies them."

Fair enough.

Magic crackled in the air, bringing with it the scent of the desert. Across from me, a man stiffened, his gaze going blank white. The room hushed, every face turned toward him.

Was he having a vision?

"Cassiopeia Clereaux." The man's voice was monotone. Every inch of him, from the sweep of his white robes to his dark hair, was deadly still. "You have come to the crossroads and succeeded, but the road becomes difficult. A great confrontation is coming. Without your magic, you will fail. Yet time is getting short to recover it. If you are smart and brave, you may prevail, but the way is growing perilous."

My heart thundered as I desperately tried to commit the seer's words to memory. The crossroads he mentioned had been foreseen by Aethelred. And his reference to a confrontation and needing my magic to survive it was exactly what Aethelred had said yesterday.

When he finished speaking, he shook his head, and his gaze cleared.

"Another one?" he asked, his voice much more animated, though vaguely confused.

"Yes, Kyros," the woman next to him said. "Quite a good one, if I do say so."

He smiled. "Excellent." His gaze met mine. "I presume it was about you? I hope it was helpful."

"It, ah…was," I said. "Though I wasn't sure I understood it all." Or maybe I had. I just didn't *want* to understand it. None of it had been good news, exactly.

"Understanding comes with time, my dear," Kyros said.

Great. With time. Just what I had tons of.

Either way, though, the locket held answers. I looked at Nuria, who held the necklace. "Will you tell me what the locket says? How to open it?"

She nodded, then bent her head. "The inscription on the front is directions for how to open the locket. I have made many in my day, and there are several different ways to get inside. Within the locket, there is something that your parents wanted you to always have."

My heart thundered, covetousness roaring. Of the thousands of times my dragon soul had coveted treasure, it had never wanted anything like this.

"How do I open it?"

"Only you are capable. You must enter the Pool of Memory. There, you will receive instructions on what to do."

"Where is the Pool of Memory?"

"Here, in the Lyceum of Metis."

Thank magic for small favors. "Could you take me to it? I'd like to do it now."

"Of course." She rose. "Come with me."

Nuria led Aidan and I through the rooms and courtyards until we reached a small building at the back of the compound. It was the oldest building by far, the stone roughhewn and ancient.

"This is why we built the Lyceum here," Nuria said. "The Pool of Memory is ancient and has been here far longer than we."

I followed her into the small building, ducking under the low doorframe to avoid hitting my head. The room lacked the many windows of the other buildings, though it was not dark. An opalescent sphere hung suspended in midair, shining a pearly light on the pool below.

The pool was a natural spring made of boulders and crystal blue water. It was a mere ten feet by ten feet and had a set of stone steps carved down into it. A small bench along the side was the only other thing in the room.

"This place is amazing," I murmured.

"It is, isn't it?" Nuria said. "You may leave your things on the bench and should enter the water with only the locket."

"And then something will happen?" I asked.

"You won't miss it." Her smile turned serious. "But do not stay too long under the water. It is wonderful, but you are subject to human physiology there as well as here. You will run out of breath if you stay too long."

I nodded. Of course I wouldn't stay 'til I drowned.

"You should wait outside," Nuria said to Aidan.

He nodded. Before he followed her out the door, he reached for my hand and pulled me to him, then pressed his lips to mine. I savored the touch before he pulled away.

"Call for me if you need me," he said. "I'll be right outside the door."

"I will." I stepped away, then watched him leave.

When I turned back to the pool, the silence made the room feel even more magical. I was surrounded by magic every day, but this was something special. An unquantifiable number of memories lay within that pool. It seemed impossible.

I hoped it wasn't.

Quickly, I toed off my boots and stripped off my clothes and dagger. I left them in a pile on the bench and approached the stairs, the locket gripped in my fist.

The water was both cool and warm at the same time, swirling around me like a living thing. It felt strange, almost like it sparkled against my skin. When I was up to my neck, the water glittered in front of my eyes like a blanket of sapphires and diamonds.

I sucked in a deep breath and submerged, the water closing over my head and sucking me into a world of eerie silence.

Memories clawed at my mind. They bombarded me from all sides, flashes of faces and names and voices that ignited the familiar headache that always came when I tried to remember my past.

I tried to choose the right one, but they all blurred. I squeezed my hand around the locket, focusing on the bite of the metal into my flesh. Suddenly, one memory gleamed clearer than the rest. I reached for it with my mind, focusing on it.

A moment later, I was standing in a small room. There was a plush blue couch and a small fireplace surrounded by bookcases. It was homey.

It was *my* home, I realized. And it was fuzzy around the edges. A memory.

I turned, feeling weightless, and caught sight of a tall man kneeling on the floor in front of a little girl who was about twelve years old. She had red hair and freckles and wore a pair of denim overalls and a rainbow shirt.

Me.

Which meant the man must be my father.

My gaze darted to him, taking in his dark hair and strong features. Familiarity burst in my mind as love exploded in my heart.

Dad.

A second later, my head throbbed painfully, a migraine on the edge of agony. It was a familiar pain. Normally, it would push me away from the memory entirely, but the Pool of Memory must be holding it at bay.

I rubbed my temples, but felt nothing. Though I moved my arm, I couldn't feel my fingertips against my temple. Because I was currently an apparition? My mind was inside this ghostly body in my old home, not in my real body back in the pool.

I tried to ignore the pain as I watched my dad speak to young me. She was so young that it was hard to think of her as myself.

"And whenever you need to return home, you use the locket." He held open his palm, and the small golden locket sat inside.

"How?" she asked.

"You press it against your heart, like this." He held the locket up and held it against his heart. "And think of your mother and me. It will open the locket."

"Okay," she said.

My dad hooked the locket around the neck of my younger self. The smile on my face was so big that I ached to be her again. But my dad's face was grim, no longer painted with a comforting smile for my younger self. Worry and concern shadowed his eyes.

Something was wrong.

Of course it was, if he was giving me a locket to help me find my way home. He feared we'd be separated.

"Okay, kiddo," he said. "What do you say we do a puzzle? Your mom will be home soon, and maybe we can surprise her with the last piece."

A memory of letting my mom put the last piece in the puzzle blasted through me, the same tearing pain that came with every other old memory I'd had since I'd awoken in the field at fifteen. I ignored the pain and watched them set up the puzzle on the coffee table in front of the fire. On the mantle behind them was a framed photo. My dad, me, and a pretty red-haired woman.

My mother. My heart ached. I'd never seen her face before.

Would she be home soon? I wanted to stick around long enough to see her. That would be okay. I'd only been here a minute.

My chest hurt as I watched. At first, I thought it was sadness. But after a moment, I realized it was lack of air.

I was drowning back in the pool.

I remembered what Aethelred had told me about the Nullifier's power. I was immortal, protected from time and decay, but not from trauma. My lungs filling with water definitely qualified as trauma.

With one last look at my dad, I pulled myself away from the vision.

Nothing happened.

My lungs continued to ache, and I was still in the living room. I tried again, closing my eyes and envisioning my body back in the pool. I strained to leave the memory, but I was caught there, held tight by invisible ropes tied tight at my arms.

Panic fluttered in my chest as wild as the pain. Something had trapped me here, inside my mind, while my body died in the Pool of Memory. My greatest fear of late had been that I'd be immortal, forced to watch my friends and family die.

Little had I known that my end would come far sooner.

My vision darkened as I struggled to escape the memory. My father and younger self blurred as I went totally blind, my consciousness floating in this strange half-world created inside my mind.

As I was about to pass out, cold water filled my mouth and swirled around my body. I thrashed and kicked, struggling to reach the surface. My toe brushed one of the rocks below, and I kicked again, catching it enough that I could push myself off.

I broke the surface with a gasp, my eyes filmed with water. I choked and blinked, trying to clear my blind eyes as I swam the short distance to the steps. As I scrambled up them, I caught sight of Aidan, straddling another figure and strangling the life out of it.

"What's—" I coughed, spitting up water. "Going on?"

Aidan jumped off the body and rushed to me, sweeping me into his arms and out of the water. His warm strength sent a rush of comfort through me.

I glanced at the body and realized it was a smoke demon. A few feet away lay a red demon, the kind who wielded a fire sword. His blade lay at his side, extinguished.

"They were trying to kill me," I murmured. "They were holding me under, weren't they?"

"Yes," Aidan said. "Victor Orriodor's seer must have found you and sent them. I heard voices and came in."

"Thank you." I kissed him hard. "I tried to escape the memory, but I couldn't."

"I'm glad I heard them."

"How did they get in? Didn't Ophelia say this place is protected?" I pushed at his chest, and he took the hint, letting me down. I knelt at the smoke demon's side and inspected him.

A charm hung around his neck. It was a simple bit of stone with a hole drilled through.

"There's one on this demon too," Aidan said from where he knelt by the other demon.

I glanced over and noticed the same charm tied around his neck. I yanked the one off the smoke demon's body, and Aidan did the same to the fire sword demon. I inspected the charm more closely, finding a strange swirled symbol carved into it.

"Penatrist charms," Aidan said. "Very rare. They allow the wearer to bypass protective spells and enter protected areas."

"Victor Orriodor is collecting all kinds of valuable charms these days."

"He is, indeed." Aidan stood. "I can't imagine he has many more of them, but we should get out of here. The seer can only see your location when your concealment charm is nullified by your fluctuating power. Let's get somewhere new and hopefully have some more time before he finds you again."

"And sends more freaking demons after me." I rose and kicked the body of the smoke demon, immediately regretting it when my toe hurt. "Why didn't he come himself?"

"Either he's busy or he doesn't want you to nullify his power."

I grinned, liking that he might be wary of me. "Let me get dressed."

Aidan glanced down, as if realizing for the first time that I was nude. Or perhaps now that I mentioned it, he felt it okay to look. His eyes darkened, but he said nothing. Smart man. He'd no doubt noticed before, but my safety had been his first concern. A girl had to like a thing like that.

I clipped the locket around my neck. "Search their pockets for transport charms. One of them should have one if they wanted to get back."

Aidan patted down the bodies as I dragged on my clothes. As I was strapping on my daggers, Aidan held up a small black stone.

"Got it. Here." He handed me the stone. "Keep it on you, in case the worst happens."

Meaning that the demons managed to get me in an unescapable position. I took the charm from him. "Thanks."

By the time I was ready, the demons had begun to disappear. They'd be nothing but a memory in a few moments.

I nudged the handle of the demon's fire sword with my toe and said, "That'd make a nice addition to my trove if I could figure out how to control the flame."

Regretfully, I turned from the blade. I didn't know how to control it, so I'd be bringing a fire hazard into my lovely trove.

Not worth the risk.

"Is that what fills your trove?" Aidan asked. "Weapons?"

"And other things." Maybe I'd show Aidan sometime, but I wasn't ready yet. Troves were personal.

"You get what you needed from your memories?" Aidan asked.

"Yeah, I think so," I said. "Let's get out of this place and find a quiet spot so I can try to open the locket. I think we've got a little while before Victor Orriodor realizes his goons have failed."

"Yes. It'd take a while to kill you. You're too tough to go easy."

I grinned. "You say the sweetest things."

"Only the truth." He held up the penatrist charm and peered at it. "And I doubt he has any more of these. They're rare enough that I've never even seen one."

"I suppose a guy in your business would want to keep track of those." Aidan ran a security company, protecting things and people for vast sums of money. Charms that could break through his work would be of definite interest to him.

"Yes. We try to keep an eye out for them on the black market. They only come up for sale once every decade or so."

"And he used two at once."

"It was good timing. You were alone and distracted. It's what I'd do. He'll probably never get a better chance." His gaze was calculating.

I'd forgotten how cunning and scary Aidan could be, since he was always on my side. But if he wanted something, he'd be ruthless in getting it. Like I was. We probably both had decent insight into Victor Orriodor's mind, though we lacked his sociopathic edge.

We left the Pool of Memory and found a nearby marble bench, shaded by a gnarled tree. Wildflowers bloomed around the base of the bench.

I took a seat and removed the locket.

"I'm going to shift," Aidan said. "To be safe."

"To better protect me."

He nodded.

"I'm figuring you out," I said.

"I don't mind." Magic swirled around him, bringing with it the sound of crashing ocean waves and the scent of the forest. A gray light glimmered, obscuring his form.

A moment later, the griffin stood in his place. His golden gaze met mine before he began to pace in a circle around the tree.

I pressed the locket to my heart and thought of my father. It was easy to think of him as I'd just seen him. Only the barest headache pinged at my mind. Perhaps because I'd already unlocked that memory.

I tried to think of my mother, but the pain came. I envisioned her face in the picture I'd seen in my memory. Her bright green eyes and red hair. My stomach churned as I poked at the corners of my mind, trying to pull on the elusive threads of memory that might lead to something more than just her face.

The scent of vanilla hit my nose. It made my heart ache and my brain throb. But it was my mother's scent. I knew it, as much from my shoddy memory as I did from the pain that indicated I was on the right track. My head only hurt when I was thinking about my past.

I held on to that scent of vanilla and the memory of my father, wishing I could see more of my mother than just a photo in my head.

Nothing came, but the locket warmed in my hand. I squeezed it tighter, thinking of my parents. Wishing I were with them.

The locket clicked in my hand, a little vibration of something opening. My eyes popped open. The memories faded. I opened my fist and looked inside.

The golden heart was cracked open at the seam. I pried it apart and peered at the interior. There was nothing but more etching, the gold incised with unfamiliar lines. I squinted, trying to make out the design.

"A map," I whispered as I stood. "It's a map."

A swirl of light surrounded Aidan, and he transformed back into himself.

"It's a map!" I held up the locket. "And it's going to take me home."

CHAPTER FIVE

"Here you go." Ophelia handed me a brass-rimmed magnifying glass.

Aidan and I had found Ophelia and Nuria after I'd made my announcement and showed her the locket. She'd taken us to an enormous library that had soaring ceilings and walls covered with massive bookcases filled with scrolls.

"It's a projecting glass," Ophelia said. "Hold the locket so that the engraved map faces the wall, then hold the glass in front of that."

I did as she said, directing the locket at a small strip of blank wall near the door. As soon as I raised the glass in front of the locket, light shined from it, projecting a series of squiggly lines on the wall.

"Wow," I said. The map was intricate and beautiful, but entirely foreign. "Where is that?"

"The outline looks like Inismor, the largest of the Arran islands," Aidan said.

"On the west coast of Ireland?" Ophelia asked.

"Yes," Aidan said.

I traced the outline of the island, searching for something familiar. On the western edge, there was a small cove. The image of soaring cliffs and a crashing cobalt sea flashed in my mind. Pain followed, an agonizing sword through my brain.

"I see it." I rubbed my temple. "An area near my house, I think."

"Where?" Aidan asked.

"There." I pointed to the little cove. A small symbol, like a flared Celtic cross inside a circle, sat right near the cove.

"Good. Then we know where to go." Aidan looked at Ophelia. "Thank you for the help."

"It is our pleasure," Nuria said. "I'd hoped Cass would never need to use the locket, but we cannot always have what we want."

Like my parents.

"Thank you." My tight throat tried to strangle the words. "Without you, I wouldn't have found my way home."

"Eventually, you would have," Nuria said. "But I'm glad I could help."

Aidan and I said our goodbyes and made our way back to the plane. The trip across the island and over the sea in our little boat was uneventful.

I hadn't yet noticed a trend with why the demons appeared when they did, and that scared me. It meant that my power was fluctuating wildly without me even knowing. Ever since I'd taken the Nullifier's power, I'd felt like a magical mess, but this confirmed it. I had no control. This wasn't normal magic I'd been saddled with.

By the time we boarded the plane, it was night again. We'd decided not to use the transport charm so that I would have it in case of emergency. I needed answers fast, but with Victor Orriodor's demons hot on my trail, I needed an escape route more.

"If the seer spots me while we're in the air, could the demons transport into the plane?" I asked.

"No," Aidan said. "I've only heard of a couple cases of supernaturals dumb enough to try to transport into a plane, and they've always missed it. Too fast for them to catch. They always end up outside, a few thousand feet back."

"And then splatted on the ground below."

"Yes."

"Good." I stared at the locket in my palm. "I'm going to try to remember my past."

I took a seat, and Aidan knelt at my knees. He was so tall that his face was still level with mine. His big hand cupped my cheek. "Are you sure? Doesn't it give you terrible headaches?"

"Yes. But I need to know what I'm walking into. And a lot of my problems now are because I don't understand where I'm from."

"Just be careful."

I nodded and leaned forward to kiss him. His hand slid from my cheek to the back of my neck, holding me firmly in place as his lips moved expertly on mine. Heat coiled low in my belly as his tongue parted my lips.

I kissed him back, throwing myself into it. If I had more time and no sword hanging over my neck, I wanted to spend a week with Aidan. Doing this. Hanging out and watching bad TV and eating take-out and doing more of this, this, this.

Regretfully, I pulled away. "As much as I'd like to continue that, my life is kinda on the line here."

He nodded ruefully. "Agreed. Be careful."

I nodded and leaned back, closing my eyes. Rustling sounded as Aidan moved away. I felt something at my waist and opened my eyes to glance down. Aidan was belting the seatbelt around my waist.

My mouth tipped up at the corner. "Thanks."

"Safety first."

"You're a good guy."

"Best you ever met." He grinned.

"Cocky."

He shrugged, his smile devastating, then turned and went to speak to the captain.

I was grinning as I closed my eyes again. For good measure, I raised the locket to my chest and pressed it against my heart, having no idea if it would work.

Everything I was doing now felt awkward and strange, like I was stumbling blind through a room looking for a key. It was there, the answers were there. I just had to find them.

But I didn't only want to find answers. I wanted to know *why* I couldn't remember. There was too much at stake, too much locked inside my mind, for me to go piecemeal, trying to remember bit by bit. I needed to know why I'd lost my memory so that maybe I could undo the damage.

I racked my brain, thinking of anything that might provide a clue. Every memory that I'd had before I was fifteen came from the nightmares that had started earlier in the summer, when Victor Orriodor had reappeared in my life.

I played the important memories over in my mind like a horrible movie, trying to reach the end where the answers lay. The memories started with Nix, Del, and me being held captive in his basement dungeon. There'd been other girls, too, who'd been taken away and not come back. And if they had come back, they'd worn collars. Those collars were the end of a girl, sapping her will and freedom, more so than even the dark cells that caged us like beasts.

I'd been taken from the cell at one point. The Monster had wanted to steal my root power. Whether he'd succeeded or not, I didn't know. My locket had protected me from dying, but my memory didn't answer whether he'd stolen my root power or destroyed it. He'd thrown me back in the cell after, a piece of trash to him.

But we'd escaped, my *deirfiúr* and I, killing a guard and racing through the dungeon to freedom. It was how I'd gotten my Mirror Mage powers, stolen straight from one of the bastards who'd imprisoned us.

When we'd reached the main floor of the Monster's home, we'd escaped out into the desert. I knew now that it wasn't any ordinary desert. It'd been a waypoint, a place between earth and the heavens and hells.

That was where my memories ended. That was where my answers had to lie. I strained to remember what happened as my *deirfiúr* and I had stood on the steps of the Monster's mansion, staring out in horror at the endless sea of sand that rolled into the distance.

Agony pierced my head as I tried to remember. I gagged and doubled over in my seat, but didn't let up. I forced my mind to stay with the memory of that moment, trying to push forward into what had happened next. Nothing came except more pain, but I continued on.

Normally, I would retreat by now, giving up on finding the memories. It was too painful. Too hopeless.

But I had no more time for hopelessness. All I had time for was perseverance and commitment.

I squeezed my eyes shut tighter and pushed into the recesses of my mind, trying desperately to remember what had happened. Sweat rolled down my face, seeping into my closed eyes and burning. Nausea rolled in my stomach, and my head grew faint.

Finally, the pain ceased. But so did everything else. Blackness consumed me.

I stumbled in the sand, my hands sinking deep into the horrible golden stuff. When I raised my head, endless hills of desert stretched ahead. Blazing sun beat upon my back.

"No, no, no." A soft, despairing voice uttered from my side.

I looked at her, the friend I'd never seen because we'd been locked in the dark the entire time we'd known each other. She was

Nix, and I recognized her only by her voice. She was skinny and pale, her haunted face framed by stringy brown hair. Despairing green eyes swept over the desert. Though she'd said she was fifteen like me, she looked a bit younger. I'd never seen her face, but she was one of my only friends in the world.

At her side, the other stood silent, horror on her face. She must be Del, my other friend. Her black hair was as limp and dirty as the other girl's, a testament to the horrifying conditions we'd lived in. But her blue eyes were determined.

More determined even than me. We'd escaped the dungeon we'd been trapped in, and this great desert wouldn't defeat us.

"Run," I said.

"But there's nowhere to go," Nix said.

"Just run." Even the desert was better than what we'd left behind. We were still on the front doorstep of the place we were trying to flee. My heart thundered, and fear clawed at my throat, sending goosebumps across my skin.

I dragged Nix to her feet, and the three of us sprinted across the sand. Sweat poured down my face and into my eyes as I raced. My bare feet burned from the hot sand. Soon, my lungs struggled to keep up. I fell to my knees, sand sticking everywhere.

My muscles ached as I struggled to my feet and continued on, falling behind the other girls. I'd been in the dungeon too long, far longer than the others. My body was too weak. I glanced behind me at the Monster's mansion. It was still so close.

I pushed myself, trying to find the strength to keep running. All it took was reminding myself what lay behind me. A sprint into barren desert was better than that.

But I kept stumbling, the heat and pain more than I could bear. I was on my knees, struggling to rise, when Nix appeared at my side. *Wordlessly, she tugged me up and pulled me with her. I leaned on her as we ran.*

When even she began to flag, Del joined our side, looping her arm around my waist. She dragged us along as we stumbled through the sand, our breathing a harsh cacophony in the quiet desert.

This time, when I looked behind me, the mansion had disappeared behind one of the dunes. But when I turned forward, all I saw was more sand. I'd never seen anything like this place. It was hell.

And I was too weak to continue on. My legs finally gave out. No matter how hard I tried, how many terrible memories of the dungeon I used to spur myself on, I couldn't move.

"Go," I said. "I will follow."

I wouldn't follow. There would be no following, not in this desert. I had no shortage of determination, but my muscles now failed. I would rather drown in sand than hold my friends back or return to the dungeon.

"No." Nix pulled at my arm. "You're coming."

"I can't walk." Tears burned my eyes, but I struggled to hold them back.

"It doesn't matter if we walk," Del said. "They can follow our tracks, and the sand goes forever. We'll never escape on foot, but we've gone as far as we need."

"There's nothing here," I said.

"We're here." She sat on the sand next to me and gestured for Nix to sit. "We're far enough from the dungeon that I can use my magic. It's no longer repressed by their spells."

"What can you do?" I asked.

"Transport."

Hope flared in my chest, a light so bright I'd swear I'd never felt it before. I could see my parents again.

She reached for our hands. I grasped hers, horrified by how bony it was. But so was mine. We'd been starving.

She closed her eyes, and her magic swelled on the air. It smelled of fresh laundry, something that made my eyes tear up for my mother.

But nothing happened.

She squeezed her eyes tighter, her magic straining, the scent strengthening.

But still, nothing happened.

Finally, she opened her eyes. "I'm not strong enough to take you both. I'm only partway through my training."

Darkness filled my chest. "Then go. Save yourself. Maybe you can send our parents back to get us."

"No." Her voice was hard as a rock. "Look around. There will be no way to find this place. You have to come with me."

"How? What will we do?"

Her gaze moved between the two of us, darkness flaring in her eyes. "Something terrible and grand."

"What is it?" Nix asked.

"I've seen my mother do it to perform great magic. Greater than she is capable of. You have to try to give me your power. Push it toward me so that I can use it to fuel my own and take you with me."

"That's not possible." I'd never heard of that. It sounded sort of like a FireSoul's magic, but not the same.

"It is for me. For my family. But it isn't free. No magic is free. You will lose something. Power, knowledge, your memory. I don't know what, but if you do this, you will be changed."

Her gaze was so serious. I looked behind, at the dune that now blocked the mansion with the dungeon. Memories of my time there welled in my mind. I didn't mind giving that up.

And if it was worse, if I gave up my magic or something else, it'd still be worth it.

"I'm in," I said.

"Me too," Nix said.

Del grasped our hands again and closed her eyes. "Envision your magic as light or sound or whatever feels natural and push it toward me."

I did as she said, envisioning my power as a golden light that I collected into a ball and shoved toward her. It didn't work at first. My magic was sticky, wanting to cling to me. But I forced it anyway, trying to give everything I had.

The scent of the other girl's magic surged on the air. Flowers. I kept my eyes squeezed tightly closed, forcing my magic toward my friend. It felt unnatural and wrong, but it was our only hope.

Energy crackled in the air. My skin tingled, as if thousands of tiny bubbles popped against my flesh. A dull noise filled my ears, and the light in front of my closed eyelids glowed brighter.

"Keep going." The dark-haired girl's voice was strained.

I shoved my magic toward her harder, desperately trying to help. We had to get out of here. Something tore deep inside of me, like my soul. It was my root power, I realized. If I kept going, I'd lose it.

But I couldn't stay here. This was our only way out, and I trusted Del. I pushed harder, urging my magic toward her.

An explosion rent the air, a noise so loud that my ears rang with it. Light flared, then everything went black. Something pulled at my body, dragging me through space and the ether until I was flung to the ground.

Pain exploded and my mind went black.

"Cass! Cass, wake up!"

Aidan's voice dragged me from the darkness. My head throbbed, and my throat was dry as the desert. I felt him unclip the seatbelt at my waist and lift me into his arms. The world spun as he carried me.

When the soft bed appeared beneath my back, I manage to pry my eyes open. I winced. Though the light was low, it still hurt my head.

"What happened?" I croaked.

"Hang on." Aidan left the room, but returned a moment later with a glass of water and a wet cloth.

Gingerly, he sat on the bed and laid the cool towel over my head. Immediately, some of the pain disappeared and I sighed.

"You passed out and started shaking, like you were having a seizure. You scared the hell out of me." Aidan looked seriously worried, his brow drawn and his eyes frightened.

"I had to know about my past."

"I know." He sighed. "That's what your locket is for. We're going to your home. Be patient. Don't hurt yourself by running into a wall."

"I can't be patient. The demons are appearing more frequently. My magic is failing. I'm a time bomb."

"You aren't. And even if your magic fails, I'm here to protect you."

"I want to protect myself."

"I know." His voice sobered. "It's one of the things I like about you. But you have friends to help you when you're down."

"I know." My dream flashed in my mind. "I do. I've had them for a long time. I remembered how I lost my memories."

"Sit up and take this painkiller first, then tell me." Gently, he helped me sit up against the pillows. Every muscle in my body ached, as if I'd actually just finished running through the desert. Or had a seizure.

I took the pill he handed me and gulped it down with cool water, then pushed my tangled hair away from my face.

"I really had a seizure?" I asked.

"Looked like it."

"I pushed at my memories until I passed out. But then I remembered what I wanted to."

"While seizing."

"Yeah. It's not a great method, I admit. But I did remember." I told him about our escape from Victor Orriodor's lair. About how Del was more than a regular transporter. About the fact that Del and Nix had also chosen their true names back in the field when we'd been fifteen. We'd thought we'd named ourselves for the stars, when in reality, these had been our names all along. And finally, that'd I'd lost my power when Del had helped us escape.

"So Victor Orriodor didn't manage to steal your power when you were fifteen," Aidan said.

Memories of the nightmare I'd had of Victor Orriodor trying to steal my root power flashed in my mind.

"Why isn't it working?" he had yelled.

The pain in my chest surged until I was certain that I was consumed by the man's gray flame. My power was waning, struggling to stay inside of me.

But I was losing it. I could feel it being peeled away. Crushed. Immolated.

Gone.

"He failed," I said. "I thought it had been him, but it wasn't. Otherwise I couldn't have given it to Del. My locket protected me, burying my power so deep inside myself that he couldn't get it." I remembered how the locket had cooled on my chest, providing relief from the pain of Victor trying to steal my power.

"Did you learn what your root power is?"

"No. I didn't think of it during the nightmare."

"But Del has it," Aidan said. "So you'll figure it out."

"I don't think she has it." I'd had a brief flare of hope when I'd thought of that, but it had dissipated quickly. "If she had it, she'd have told me."

But what had happened to it? I shivered. "Do you think it's gone forever?"

"No." The certainty in his voice made me feel a bit better. "Del's talent is rare. I've never heard of a supernatural doing that before. If she can do that, anything is possible. Which means getting your magic back is possible."

I hoped he was right. I'd wanted answers so badly, but now that I was getting them, I didn't like what I was learning.

CHAPTER SIX

I spent the remainder of the plane ride resting, the locket gripped in my fist. It'd be less weird to wear it around my neck, but for some reason, holding it in my hand was more comfortable.

By the time we landed on the tiny airstrip at Inismor, my headache had dissipated entirely. Whatever Aidan had given me for it had been strong.

The wind was brisk and the night dark when we climbed down the steps from the plane. Moonlight shined on the land, revealing fields bisected by low stone walls. No mountains on Inismor and hardly any trees—this island was just a flat stretch of rock that jutted out from the sea.

On the tarmac, which was little more than a narrow paved road with nothing but us and the plane, Aidan glanced at his watch. "It's after ten."

"Where's the car?" I asked, then laughed. "Wow, I've really gotten used to traveling with you, haven't I?"

"What do you mean?"

"Normally, I'd get off the plane with all the other plebeians and shuffle my way to the bus stop or car rental desk. I've only been traveling with you for a little over a month, and I'm already used to seeing a luxury vehicle waiting for me when I disembark."

He grinned. "Inismor doesn't have any of those. And transportation is coming."

"Well, good, because I'm spoiled and expect only the best." I was joking, but Aidan's nod looked serious.

I was about to tell him that I'd need to call Del and Nix to tell them what I'd learned when the clip-clop of horse's hooves on pavement sounded. I turned to see two big horses each pulling an open wagon.

My friend were sitting in the backs of the wagons—Del, Nix, Connor, and Claire. My heart leapt, but it was followed quickly by worry. The traps pulled to a stop in front of us.

"What are you guys doing here?" I asked Del and Nix. "You're supposed to be in Magic's Bend."

Del hiked her thumb at Aidan. "He called us." Said your concealment charm is really going to shit and you needed backup."

Worry gnawed in my chest. "But you're at risk now."

"We were always at risk," Nix said. "As long as Victor Orriodor is alive."

"Maybe so." I pointed at Connor and Claire, our two friends who owned Potions & Pastilles, followed her. "But they weren't."

"You think we'd leave you hanging?" Connor asked. His dark hair flopped over his brow, and his black band t-shirt blended with the night.

"We've had this talk before," Claire said as she shoved her long brown hair back from her face. She was wearing black like her brother, but it was all leather. She'd come dressed in her best demon-hunting wear. "So don't be dense. We have your back."

I smiled. "Thanks, guys. I just don't want you to get hurt."

"Demons could pop out of the air at any second and try to off you," Claire said. "We need to be here to kick their asses."

"Thanks." I hugged each of them fiercely. Except for Connor, who had a full satchel hanging at his side. That would be full of potion bombs, and I didn't want to jostle it. Him, I hugged lightly.

"So you've found your childhood home?" Nix asked. There was joy in her voice, but also the slightest tinge of envy. I didn't blame her. I'd feel it, too, in her position. None of us liked not knowing our histories.

"In theory," I said. "We know it should be, at least."

"Then lead on." Del gestured to the wagons.

"This is our transportation?" I asked.

"Pony traps," Aidan said. "Inismor only has a few cars, and they're all owned by locals."

"But you can rent pony traps." Nix hopped into one of the traps. "Thanks, Fergus."

The driver nodded, then tipped his cap to Aidan.

"Seriously?" I asked. "We're kind of in a hurry."

"Faster than walking," Del said as she climbed into another trap. Connor and Claire followed her in. "And I can't transport this many people."

That was what she thought. After my most recent vision, I'd bet there was a way.

"The island is small," Aidan said.

The two drivers were old men with white hair and tweed caps. They looked as Irish as shamrocks. They were supernaturals of some kind, but I didn't know which. According to what Aidan had said, there were only two hundred inhabitants on Inismor, and all were Magica or Shifter.

Aidan and I climbed into the trap with Nix.

"Did you find out why Victor Orriodor was on the stage at the memorial? Is he part of the order?" I asked.

"No," Nix said. "We spoke to Dr. Garriso, who asked around for us, but he knew nothing. Aerdeca and Mordaca also haven't come up with anything yet."

"Damn," I muttered. Whatever Victor was up to, it made my skin prickle with goosebumps.

"Where to?" Fergus asked. His Irish accent was thick.

"West side of the island," Aidan said. "Near Dún Dúchathair. There's a lane that leads to a house."

"Aye, I know it."

"Dún Dúchathair?" I asked as the trap started to move, its wheels crunching on the gravel road.

"I did some research while you were asleep," Aidan said. "I think your family home is located near an Iron Age fort named Dún Dúchathair. The Black Fort."

"To the Black Fort, then," I said. That didn't sound ominous at all.

It only took twenty minutes of bumping along a gravel road to reach the end of the lane. We'd passed by several small farms and a pub sitting in the middle of nowhere that had been bursting with light and the sound of fiddles. But by the time we reached our stopping point, we were alone in the silent, dark night.

Fergus halted the trap and said, "Here's where I leave you. Molly can't go any farther."

I squinted past him, toward the sea. The moon lit a narrow lane, barely wide enough for a cart like Molly's.

"Is it protected?" I asked.

"Aye, that it is. Good luck gettin' past. No one's been there in years."

Since my parents. "Thank you."

I swung my small duffle over my shoulder and climbed out of the cart behind Aidan. He paid the driver while I started up the lane. I couldn't see what was at the end, though the distant sound of crashing waves suggested that we were near the cliffs.

Goose bumps rose on my skin as I walked, my feet crunching on the gravel. I was so close to my family home, but I couldn't decide if it felt familiar. I hated that.

The land all around was flat, covered in slabs of broken rock. Scrubby grass peeked through the stone sheets, but this was no place that a person could till a field. It was a surreal landscape.

Why had my parents lived in such a remote area?

"Cass!" Nix called. "Little help here, please!"

I turned. My friends stood in a group about twenty feet back. Aidan and Connor each held a handle of a massive cooler, and everyone else had a small duffle slung over their shoulders, but otherwise they didn't have too much to carry.

What did they need help with?

"The barrier?" Del said. "We can't cross it."

"Oh!" I must have passed it and not realized. I hurried toward them.

Nix placed her hand on the invisible magical barrier. She looked like a mime.

I held out a hand to Nix, and she grasped it. I tried to pull her through, hoping that my touch would indicate to the protective spell that she was allowed to pass.

"Ow!" Nix yanked her hand from mine and jumped back. "That's not going to work."

"I have the penatrist charms," Aidan said. "We can come through one at a time."

I nodded and stepped back. Aidan dug into a pocket, then handed a charm over to Connor. They walked through the barrier without incident. Aidan set the cooler on the ground, then took the charm from Connor and handed them over to Nix and Claire. They crossed and Del joined them a moment later.

"Those are some scary charms," Del said.

"That they are," Aidan said. "And rare as dragons. Though we did meet a few last week."

I thought of the tiny dragons I'd met in Switzerland last week. Fire, water, air, and stone. I'd love to see them again.

I turned and headed up the lane, not bothering to ask if everyone was ready to go. My ability to be polite had fled with the arrival of my anxiety over seeing my old home.

When it appeared ahead, a moderately-sized stone house at the edge of the cliff, my heart felt like it contracted. The door was red. Window boxes were barren, but hinted at my family's love for gardening. I climbed up the three stone steps and touched the smooth red paint, waiting for memories to come.

None did.

When I poked around inside my head, trying to recall any, only the pain came. I winced and removed my hand from the door.

Everyone else was silent, which was damned unusual for our group. I guess they sensed this was kind of a big deal. I hated to be all dramatic about it, though. Moping and being serious would get me nowhere. If I was going to grieve for what I'd lost, it wouldn't be now.

"I hope you brought some PBR in that cooler," I said as I turned the doorknob. The words came out more awkwardly than I'd hoped, but they did the trick. They broke the solemnity.

"Better believe it," Connor said. "Del and Nix said we were coming to help you on some abandoned island, and I knew I had to be prepared."

"You're a treasure."

Connor was a hearth witch, his talents lying in the domestic arts. Though he did have a mean hand with potions and could whip up a deadly spell in an instant. It made him as dangerous as his Fire Mage sister, though in a subtler way.

I stepped into the front hall, which was a simple space with a wooden floor and high ceiling. A painting of cliffs was hung on the far wall, with doors bracketing either side.

We set up shop in the kitchen, a homey room with warm wooden cabinets and an old cast iron stove. Electricity no longer worked, but the rest of the house had been preserved in good condition, most likely by the protective spell. There was little dust, and everything was put away neatly.

Like my parents had just disappeared one day.

Through the faint buzzing in my head, I could hear Connor and Claire unloading the cooler with goodies they'd brought from P & P.

Nix and Del appeared on either side of me and clasped my hands.

"How're you doing?" Del asked softly.

"All right." I stared blindly at the black window, my throat tight with unshed tears. "My parents are dead."

"I'm sorry," Nix said.

"Me too," Del said.

"That makes three of us." I squeezed their hands. Besides Del and Nix, the closest thing I had left to living kin were the dragonets I'd met last week. "But I've got you guys and we're family."

"You do. Always," Del said.

"I'm sorry I've been totally self-absorbed lately," I said. "I know I'm lucky to be getting answers about my past. That's more than…" I trailed off, not knowing how to finish that statement. It sounded awful.

"That's more than what we've got, is what you mean," Del said.

"Yeah. But I'll help you find answers if you want them."

"I do," Del said. "But I've accepted that I won't get them. Not unless they come to me."

"Same," Nix said. "We've all looked on and off in the past, but had no luck. Now they're falling into your lap, and they're not good."

"No, they're not," I said.

They squeezed my hands.

"I learned how we lost our memories. And how I lost my power."

"Yeah?" Intrigue colored Del's voice.

I explained my dream, how Del's transport power was stronger than we'd realized.

"My mother could do magic like that?" Del asked. "*I* could do magic like that?"

"Yeah. I guess you forgot how when we blasted all our memories away."

"Must have been a strong spell for that to happen," Nix said.

I remembered the blazing light and sound. "Strongest I've ever felt. Transporting from a waypoint without a portal is pretty insane, really."

"Yeah," Del said. "That's some badass power. Maybe I do want to learn more."

I reached for the locket around my neck, taking comfort from the metal. "At the end, when I was afraid you wouldn't have enough power to get us out of there, I gave up my root power. I pushed it toward you."

"What?" Del demanded. "You gave it up? What was it?"

"I don't know what it was. I just thought of it as *my power*. Not what the gift actually was. But I was terrified of having to stay there. So I pushed it toward you. Then it was gone." I tried to ignore the fear that it could be gone forever.

"I don't feel it inside me, though," Del said. "At least, I don't think."

"Yeah, I know," I said. "Otherwise you would have told me. So if you don't have it, where did it go?"

"I don't know," Del said.

"I don't think I gave up mine," Nix said. "But I have no idea."

"Whatever it is, we'll figure it out," Del said. "We'll get your power back. Then you can go back to raiding tombs and being mortal like the rest of us."

I thought of the demons trying to drown me in the Pool of Memory. "I'm not that immortal."

"Immortal enough," Nix said. "I'd rather you die of old age, happily watching sitcoms with your eighty grandkids."

I laughed. "I don't know if that's in my future, but it sounds traumatizing to the kids. And I was envisioning cats, anyway."

"Yeah, you have a point." Del tugged on my hand so that I turned to face the group. "Let's have a beer."

"Good idea," I said. "We'll eat, get a bit of rest, and get an early start to explore this place at dawn."

Part of me wanted to do it now, but it was pitch black outside. And honestly, I needed a bit of time to decompress and get my head on straight. Being here threw my whole system out of whack, and my mind felt like it was running a million miles a minute all while standing still.

Aidan handed me a PBR and a ham sandwich, and I took them gratefully.

As I ate and drank in the little kitchen where I'd been raised, the sound of my friends and family filled the empty space in my heart. I still ached for what I'd lost, and still didn't remember enough, but I was grateful for what I had.

That night, Aidan and I slept in one of the guest bedrooms. I'd made Del go upstairs and explore, finding which rooms had been my parents' and mine so that I didn't go into them tonight. I couldn't face it yet, and I didn't want to cry any more.

Despite my best intentions, I cried myself to sleep anyway. But at least Aidan was there to hold me.

"Right, folks, let's Sherlock Holmes the hell out of this place," I said before polishing off the last of my coffee.

As I'd hoped, I'd woken feeling a hell of a lot better. With the dawn light shining through the windows, everything looked a bit more positive. Claire and Connor had made us a quick breakfast of leftover pastries and coffee, and we were ready to start the day.

"So, what do we do?" Claire asked.

"I need to figure out what my root power was. Maybe I can get it back."

"Both sound good."

Yeah, at this point, I'd take either. "I know that my locket has something to do with my root power because it protected me when Victor Orriodor tried to steal my root power when I was fifteen. And the locket had a map that led me here. So, let's look for clues. Any kind of clue."

At this point, I wasn't super picky. I just needed info.

"Let's start in the house, then," Del said. "Everyone in a different room."

We stood and everyone slowly filed out the door. When they were all gone, Aidan grabbed my hands and met my gaze.

"You doing okay?" Concern creased his brow.

"Yeah. I am. Really. I just needed a bit of a cry to get rid of the initial shock. Now I'm good to go."

It wouldn't be easy to deal with it all, but I could handle it now. I wished I were the sort to immediately tough out the bad stuff, but life's hardballs sometimes made me curl up in a ball for a little while before I could deal with them. I was a real badass underneath my hard shell, clearly.

"Good." Aidan kissed my forehead and I smiled. "Let's get started."

We searched the house for an hour, but it didn't take me long to figure out that there was probably nothing here amongst the photos and books that I longed to explore more fully. I'd started to, but tears had blinded me by the third photo I'd looked at. Though they painted a picture of my life here, they didn't provide information about my root power. And it was just too painful to look at them now. Too painful to be in this house.

I'd come back and do it one day, but not now.

"I'm headed outside," I said.

Del looked up from where she was sorting through some pretty wooden boxes. "Should we come?"

"Whenever you're done there." I wanted some time to myself.

And though I was glad my friends were here, I doubted they'd be the ones to find the clue. I barely understood what we were looking for, so my only hope was that I would recognize it when I saw it.

The sun shone brightly when I walked outside, and I could smell the fresh salt air of the sea. Gray stone slabs dotted the landscape, with grass poking up between the crevices. The land dropped off about fifty yards in front of the house, going straight down into the dark blue sea. There was nothing sticking out of the land—no trees or other houses.

I closed my eyes and sucked in a deep breath, trying to feel or smell any nearby magic. It was as good a place as any to start. At first, all I smelled was the ocean. But after a moment, I got a whiff of power. Something ancient. I couldn't have described the smell for a million dollars, but it evoked thoughts of battle and life and death.

I opened my eyes and followed it, scrambling over the strange flat rocks as I headed diagonally away from the house, toward the sea to the south. The land undulated, small hills of rock concealing and revealing the landscape ahead.

When a massive, black stone wall appeared in the distance, I gasped. It was huge, built of millions of stones, and curved back toward the sea. The ancient power radiated from the wall.

I hurried toward it, stumbling on the slabs of rock but unable to take my gaze from the wall. The top was broken and jagged, as if the stones had slowly fallen away in the thousands of years since it had been built. It was still over fifty feet tall, however.

Both ends of the wall terminated at the cliff that plunged into the sea. It must have protected a jutting piece of land, using the sea as its back wall.

As I neared it, the prickle of protection charms skittered across my skin. This place was even more locked down than my family's home. Anyone who intended me harm wouldn't be getting through here, I'd bet.

There was no door, so I began to climb, sticking my fingers in the crevices between the rocks. The wall was so ancient that there was no mortar, which made it easier to find a hand hold.

When I neared the top, a rock wobbled beneath my toe. My heart jumped into my chest as I scrambled away, seeking solid footing. By the time I crawled onto the top of the wall, which was at least twenty feet across, my heart pounded and sweat dripped down my sides.

I lay on the top, catching my breath. This stone wall made the ones surrounding castles look like a joke.

When I could breathe again, I clambered across the top of the wall to the other side. The stone beneath my feet was loose—filler rock, I thought it was called.

At the other side, I looked out at the land. As I'd expected, there was an expanse of grass about the size of a football field that plunged into the sea on the other side. Whoever had built this wall thousands of years ago had been hiding from something.

My gaze roved over the grass within, which was scattered with wildflowers instead of the slabs of stone that covered the ground outside of the wall. In the middle of the space was a stone circle. Within, three tall white statues stood in an arc. My heart thundered.

They were important. My now-dormant dragon sense roared within my chest, trying to break past the Nullifier's magic. It responded to anything of great value, and this place was so important that it was making my dragon sense fight the Nullifier's power.

I needed to get closer. With shaking hands, I climbed down the wall. The sun beat upon my back as I raced across the grass toward the statues.

Magic thrummed in the air as I neared them, and my skin prickled. Strength filled my limbs as I entered the circle. The boundary stones were white, which was strange. Stone circles in Ireland and the nearby UK were often gray granite or some other kind of boring rock. These were a beautiful, gleaming white.

But it was the statues that caught my eye. They stood in an arc, facing a large, round stone disk set in the middle of the circle. Three women, each in elegant robes.

Their features were simple, not easily recognizable as any one person.

I walked up to the nearest one, who was surrounded by stone animals. Deer, rabbits, a badger, and birds. Unable to help myself, I reached out and touched her hands, which were folded in front of her body.

The stone was warm beneath my fingertips, and the strangest feeling shot up my arm. Warmth, strength, life—all flowed through me. The world felt clearer and sharper, and I felt more alive than I ever had. Like the air itself gave me power. My hand seemed to glow where it lay over hers.

Reluctantly, I pulled my hand away and looked at it. The glowing had ceased.

Weird.

I moved on to the next statue. Her face was narrow, cheekbones protruding. The hands that peeked out from her robe were almost bony. I reached out to touch one, but yanked my hand back almost immediately after touching the cold stone. One brief touch had sucked the strength from me. My knees felt weak.

Was the first statue life, and this one death?

I glanced at the last statue, then approached it. She looked like a normal woman. No skeletal hands or animals at her side. Despite her simplicity, I was drawn to her in a way that I hadn't been with the others.

My hand shook as I reached out to touch her. As soon as I made contact with the stone, I gasped. Magic flowed through me, strong and fierce. It made my skin tingle and my heart soar.

A light appeared at the statue's side. The glow coalesced into the shape of a woman. I squinted at her. After a moment, the features became clearer, the body more solid. Magic flowed from her, a bright light that glittered gold.

She looked a bit like me. But older. Just like the woman from the photos in my house.

My heart leapt. "Mom?"

She smiled. "Cass."

I reached out to hug her, but my arms passed through her ghostly body. "You aren't real."

I knew it, but it was hard not to tear up at the knowledge.

"Not the way that you are, no."

"What happened to you and Dad?" My throat tightened on the words.

"I am here because we are no longer with you. I had wanted to explain to you in person when you grew up. But that was not possible."

"Why?"

"I am not here for that. I am here to explain what you are."

"What I am?"

"Part of the Triumvirate." She motioned to the three statues. "Triumvirate is from Latin. Three of power. You are one of the three."

I glanced up at the statue I stood near. "That's me? And Del and Nix are the others?"

"Yes. You were prophesied. Along with Del and Nix. A balance of life, death, and magic embodied by the three supernaturals who are worthy. Del is in the middle, Nix at the end."

"Whoa."

My mother smiled. "Take the portal to the League of FireSouls. They will help you."

"League of FireSouls?"

She pointed to something behind me and said, "That portal."

I turned to see that she indicated the circular stone slab set into the ground in front of the statues.

When I spun back to face her, she had faded slightly. The magical aura that had surrounded her was also dissipating. "I love you, Cass. I will always love you."

"I love you, too."

By the time I'd finished speaking, she had disappeared. Whatever spell had powered the apparition of my mother, it had run out of juice.

I swallowed hard against the tears that threatened to rise, forcing them down. I didn't have time for a good cry right now.

"Cass!" Nix's voice sounded from the distance.

I turned. She stood on top of the wall, waving. Claire joined her a moment later. They must be using the penatrist charms to get through the protections, coming over the wall one at a time.

Nix and Claire tossed their charms to the others, then climbed down from the wall and hurried across the grass toward me. The other's followed.

"What is this place?" Nix asked when she stopped. Her gaze was drawn to the statue of the bony woman.

"The magic here is strong," Claire said.

Del joined us. "That's an understatement."

"This is us." I indicated the statues. "The middle one is Del."

"Death?" Nix asked.

"Yeah, how'd you know?"

"She looks like the freaking crypt keeper."

Del punched her in the shoulder.

I laughed. "Well, it helps explain your phantom side, Del."

"You're standing near that one," Nix said. "So I assume I'm the Disney princess with all the animal friends?"

"Yep," I said.

She shrugged. "Won't say no to that. Especially if they wanted to clean my apartment. But if Del is death, what am I? Animal whisperer?"

"Life." I looked at my statue. "And I'm magic, whatever the heck that means." I explained to them what the apparition of my mother had said about the League of FireSouls and the portal.

"We should go now," Del said.

I nodded. "But only the FireSouls."

"Not a chance," Aidan said.

"If this is the organization that Ophelia was talking about, they won't take kindly to outsiders knowing what they are. At least Del, Nix, and I are the same as they are. We can't rat them out to the Order of the Magica without getting ourselves in trouble, too."

"Still, not going to happen. I'm not leaving your side." Aidan's face was set.

I went to him, putting my hand on his arm. The muscles were corded with tension. "They might not see us if we come with an outsider. I promise I'll call you on my comms charm if we need help. But I really, really need these answers."

"I just want you to be safe."

"I've been protecting myself for most of my life. And I'm damned good at it." I squeezed his arm.

"You don't have your magic."

"I didn't use my magic for most of my life, either. And I have Del and Nix."

"Grim Reaper, at your service." Del saluted.

Nix punched her and hissed, "Be serious."

"And don't get cocky," I said. "You're not the Grim Reaper."

"I could be." She waggled her brows.

"And maybe that's what we'll find out. But we need to go alone." I turned back to Aidan. "I promise I'll call you if I need you."

Indecision warred on his face.

"I need these answers, Aidan. I can't risk them clamming up because we brought an outsider."

He nodded jerkily, his face tight. But it was hard to fight my logic. I leaned up and pressed a quick kiss to his cheek, then turned to Connor and Claire.

"Thank you for coming, guys. I think you can go home now, though."

"We'll sort it out," Claire said. "Now get going. There are answers waiting for you."

I wasn't sure what she meant by *sort it out*, but she was right. There were answers waiting, and I was dying to get to them.

CHAPTER SEVEN

I stepped back from Aidan and turned to Del and Nix. "Ready?"

"Like a cat's ready for tuna," Del said.

We walked to the round stone disk and stood around it in a circle, linking hands.

"Step on it on the count of three," I said.

They nodded.

I took one last glance at Aidan, whose face was worried, then raised my foot and counted down.

When I stepped on the stone, an invisible force grabbed me around the waist and sucked me into the ether. The world went black for a fraction of a second.

When the light came back, I found myself standing in a beautiful glen. A burbling river tumbled along beside us, and massive trees soared overhead, shielding us. I let go of Del's and Nix's hands and spun in a circle, but all I saw was forest. No roads or signs or anything.

"Guess we have to find it," Nix said.

"Makes sense," I said. What better way to prove you were a FireSoul than to use your dragon sense to find what you sought? "But you'll have to do the honors, seeing as I'm currently a dud."

Nix nodded and closed her eyes. Her magic swelled in the air, the scent of flowers rising.

She opened her eyes. "Follow the river upstream."

We set off along the riverbank, hopping over massive boulders covered in moss. Clusters of violets grew at the base of the big, old trees.

"Very fairytale-esque, isn't it?" Del said.

A flash of red caught my eye, and I turned my head. Something fluttered in the trees in the distance. Just a bird. But I squinted at it anyway, an odd familiarity tugging at me.

It flew closer, flapping brilliant red wings and sporting an oddly long neck. A little puff of flame escaped its mouth.

That was no bird.

My heart leapt. "Dragonets!"

The fire dragonet flew toward me, followed by the sparkling blue water dragonet. They hovered around my head and I laughed. A moment later, the smoky gray form of the air dragonet appeared, followed by the stone dragonet. They were the size of cats, but were far more deadly.

"Who are these guys?" Del asked.

"My dragonet friends. I met them in the forest in Switzerland. They lived near the Nullifier, who told me that they are made of magic rather than flesh and blood."

"Maybe that's why they're here." Nix held out a hand so that the fire dragonet could sniff her. "This place is all magic."

"Maybe." I looked at the water dragonet who glittered blue as the Caribbean sea. "Will you accompany us?"

The dragonet nodded its head and turned to zoom off down the river. We continued on our way, the dragonets zipping around us. As we walked, the residual magic in the air grew stronger. It prickled against my skin, the magic of dozens of supernaturals or one really powerful magical hotspot. Whatever it was, we'd be outnumbered, power-wise.

"I think we're getting close," Nix said. "Feel that?"

"Yeah."

Just ahead, a small round stone tower with a slate roof crouched near the river. Vines crawled up the side, sprouting red roses all the way up to the top. Nothing impressive, but it was the first structure we'd seen.

"I hope your dragonet buddies give us some cred," Del muttered.

"That depends." A deep voice sounded from in front of us. A figure stepped out from behind the small tower. He was as tall as Aidan, with dark skin and a warrior's face. Hard eyes, strong jaw, and a scar across his cheek that was dashing rather than disfiguring. He wore burnished red leather armor and had a long sword slung at his side.

"Meow," Del whispered at my side.

I elbowed her. He was good-looking, but not worth pissing off with cat calls.

"The dragonets are selective," he said. "But they've been known to be mistaken. Who are you?"

"Cassiopeia Clereaux," I said. It hurt too much to try to use my family's given name.

"Phoenix Knight," Nix said.

"Delphine Hally, at your service."

I couldn't tell, but I thought her eyebrows waggled.

Moron. Just because he was handsome didn't mean he wouldn't stab us with his sword. I tried to pick up his magical signature, sniffing subtly and focusing on my other senses.

When I got a whiff of smoke and something burning, I relaxed a bit. We'd found the FireSouls, at least. Other magical signatures smelled like smoke, but since we were on the FireSouls' land, I felt safe assuming he was one of us. Hopefully they wouldn't hurt their own kind. And my mother *had* sent me here. I trusted her.

"We're looking for the League of FireSouls," I said.

"I know. I am Alton, one of their number. We have been expecting you."

"Really?"

He inclined his head. "Eventually. It was prophesied that the Triumvirate would come to us."

Del made a doubtful face and pointed to herself, then me and Nix. "Us?"

"Indeed. But you are not… what I expected."

"Sorry to disappoint," I said.

"Hardly. Come, we will go to the sanctuary." He turned and started down the river.

I glanced at Del and Nix, who shrugged, and we followed. The dragonets kept pace beside me, zipping between the trees and diving over the river.

Alton's strides were long as he cut through the forest. I hurried to catch up, glancing at his hard eyes to find them glued on the path ahead.

"Why are the dragonets here when they were just in Switzerland last week?" I asked.

He looked down at me quickly, then back at the forest. "Switzerland is the home of dragons. One of them, at least."

"Dragons are dead."

"Maybe. But the dragonets like it there anyway. But they also like FireSouls. We're their next closest kin. So they come here."

I looked around at the enchanted forest. "Where is here, exactly?"

"A protected part of the Arcadian forest, part of an abandoned waypoint."

Great. Another waypoint.

A gray stone wall appeared through the trees, distracting me.

"Is this it?" Del asked from behind.

"It is," Alton said.

We neared it, and I had to crane my neck to see to the top. "It's huge."

"A relic of the past, when our numbers were greater," Alton said. "Though we still needed sanctuary then, too."

Upon closer inspection, I realized that the top of the ramparts was a bit worn down and the ivy that grew up the side of the wall had a wild look rather than a cultivated one. Above the great wooden gate, there were two cutouts at the top of the wall where guards could stand. But they were empty.

The forest floor gave way to packed dirt ground only twenty feet in front of the gate. No road or anything. Just forest, then fortress.

Alton approached the gate and pressed his hand to a round stone that protruded from the wall. Magic sparked in the air and tingled against my skin as the wooden gate slowly creaked upward. The dragonets flew through.

"Come." Alton stepped back and gestured to the gate.

We walked through ahead of him, into a massive courtyard. Twisty towers and turrets and ornate buildings filled the space, like something out of a fairytale. Flowering vines crawled up the sides, reaching for tall balconies that overlooked the forest. The dragonets perched among the vines, bright spots of color that looked like large flowers. Grass grew wild between the pathways, and fountains ran dry. Birds chirped and sang.

But it was empty. The fortress should have held hundreds. Instead, there was no one. Even the heavy cloak of magic that fell over the place felt stale.

This was where I'd come for all my answers?

"What happened to the League of FireSouls?" I asked.

"Nothing good," Del muttered.

I turned to see Alton walking toward us as the wooden gate closed behind us. "Eleven years ago, we picked the wrong fight."

"Why?" Nix asked.

"It was the only fight." He rubbed his face as if he were exhausted. "The necessary fight."

I waited for him to say more. He didn't.

"That's all pretty cryptic," I said.

"I don't think it's the place to start the story," Alton said.

"Alton!"

I turned toward the voice. A tall figure hurried from one of the towers in the center of the courtyard. She wore jeans and a paint-splattered t-shirt and looked to be about our age. Her magic cloaked her like armor, looking almost like a pale gray light shrouding her body.

"Corin," Alton said. "The Triumvirate has arrived. Gather the others. We'll meet at the river."

Corin nodded and raced off.

"Do you get the feeling they think we're more important than we actually are?" Del whispered.

"Yeah." The Triumvirate sounded very fancy and very powerful.

We were neither. Moderately powerful, perhaps, but certainly not fancy.

"Come." Alton started for the far back corner of the compound.

We followed. My gaze darted all over the place, looking for more FireSouls. I found none.

Alton led us down winding stone paths between the buildings. I expected Merlin to jump out at any moment, but he didn't. Nor did anyone else.

The sound of a burbling river drew my gaze forward. The buildings ended, and the path led to a clearing covered in grass. A narrow river cut across, with more grass and the wide stone wall on the other side. It flowed out through a hole at the base of the wall. Metal grates protected the opening where the river flowed out, keeping anyone from climbing in.

"Take a seat." Alton gestured to the stone benches positioned beneath flowering trees. Sun sparkled through the leaves, casting dappled shade.

We sat, the three of us on a bench near the edge.

"We used to meet in the Council Room, but there are no longer enough of us to fill the table," he said.

I was about to ask how many there were when people started to arrive and sit on the benches. They came quickly, one after the other, until a group of eight filled the clearing. They were all ages and races, some dressed for war, like Alton, and others in casual clothes like Corin. Each had a magical signature that was distinctly FireSoul and obviously powerful.

Anytime I met one's eyes, they smiled. I smiled back, bemused.

"Right, we're all here," Alton said. "From left to right, we have Kade, Phoebe, Mack, Corin, Castille, Luna, Calpheus, and Brunel. Our librarian, Flora, does not like to leave her books."

They all nodded as their names were called. I waved.

"And here we have Cassiopeia Clereaux, Phoenix Knight, and Delphine Hally. The Triumvirate."

"About bloody time," Mack muttered. He was a mountain of a man, with thick auburn hair and a hard face.

"In our defense, we didn't know we were the Triumvirate until this morning," Del said.

"And we're still not sure what that is," I said. "Or what you guys are, exactly. The ghost of my dead mother told me to come here, but beyond that, I'm at a loss."

"Alice McFane." Mack said her name with heaviness. Respect. He bowed his head.

I liked him already.

"We are what remains of the League of FireSouls," Alton said. "The League was formed hundreds of years ago to protect our kind from persecution."

"At the hands of the Order of the Magica or the Alpha Council," I said.

"Yes. They don't understand our kind, or realize that most of us don't intend to use our power for harm."

"Terrified bigots, the lot of them," Mack grumbled.

Alton inclined his head. "They've had good reason to fear us in the past. FireSouls who went rogue. The League was formed in response to the rise of a powerful, evil FireSoul. Protecting ourselves sometimes means policing ourselves. Stopping rogue FireSouls from harming others and giving us a bad name is a large part of what we try to do."

"Our name is still bad, though," Del said. "We've been hiding from the Order of the Magica and the Alpha Council for years because of what we are."

"Yes. It doesn't take much to make people fear us. We once had an alliance with the Order of the Magica. If we kept the FireSouls in line, they would not hunt us. But that has been gone for generations, and we no longer hold any sway with them. They capture and imprison FireSouls."

"What about the Alpha Council?" I asked, remembering the FireSoul prisoner I'd seen at the Alpha Council headquarters a month ago. The Shifter's government was separate from the Magica's government, but they still hunted FireSouls.

"They are worse," Alton said. "Because they are not Magica, and FireSouls are always Magica, they are even less trusting of them. We have never been able to form an agreement with the Alpha Council."

"They captured a FireSoul about a month ago," I said. "I saw him in their headquarters at Glencarrough."

"We know. We have been planning a rescue, but those so rarely work. We will try anyway."

"You try to rescue the FireSouls held at the Prison for Magical Miscreants?"

"We do, though we are not often successful. The protections are too great at the prison. But we try. With our decreased numbers, it is one of the few things we can do to help our kind."

Wow. These guys were like heroes or something. All Nix, Del, and I had ever done was run and lay low and accumulate our hordes. I suddenly felt like a selfish slacker.

"Were my parents part of this?"

"Yes," Alton said. "Ethan and Alice McFane were two of our leaders."

"You came here once when you were an infant," an older man said. Though his dark skin was creased with lines and his hair turned partially white, he had the bearing of a warrior, and wisdom radiated from him. I thought his name was Castille. "But once you were born, the McFanes decided they wanted to give you a normal life. As best they could. So they bought the house on Inismor."

"Why there? It's so barren."

"The Black Fort holds powerful magic," Castille said. "Ancient magic that is thousands of years old. It was one of the few places strong enough to support an Everlong Portal like the one that is currently there. And it provides protection."

"And the statues? This whole Triumvirate business?" Del asked. "What's all that about?"

"According to legend, you three were prophesied," Alton said.

"By who?"

"An ancient seer, long dead. Her prophecy was recorded on the walls of a passage tomb in central Ireland."

At my confused look, he said, "A chambered cairn, some call them."

Ah, right. "But passage tombs are over five thousand years old."

I'd never been inside one of the massive piles of stone that had rooms built inside. They often looked like nothing more than small, odd hills. Their secrets lay within, but they'd never had anything to tempt me. "Writing didn't exist then."

"Not as we know it, no. But the seer's message has been passed down for generations. We didn't know when the Triumvirate would arrive, only that they were the physical manifestations of the balance between life, death, and magic. And that they would be faced with a great task."

"A series of tasks," Castille added.

"Great," Del muttered.

"One for each?" Nix asked.

"We think," Alton said. "But we do not know. That is for you to find out. We believe you must fight something greater than yourself."

"I need my magic if I'm to accomplish some great task," I said. The hollowness inside me felt even wider now that I knew I had some prophesied great task to accomplish. Without my power, I couldn't handle my own life recently, much less a *Great Task*.

"And what about the statues at the Black Fort?" Nix asked. "Were they built there? Did my parents live near there?"

"And mine?" Del asked.

"I am sorry, but we do not know about either of your parents," Castille said. "Those statues were not built by human hands. When the McFanes moved to Inismor, the statues formed there. By magic, we believe, because they never saw anyone go to the Black Fort and erect them. It's as if the place were waiting for your arrival, Cassiopeia."

"Whoa, slow down." This was getting a lot more serious than I'd anticipated. "It sounds like you're saying I'm some kind of chosen one."

"And Del and Nix." Alton gestured to them.

"I don't think we're qualified," Del said.

"I agree." I nodded vigorously.

"Other people disagree," Alton said. "Victor Orriodor is one of them."

"Him? What do you know about that bastard?" I asked.

"He is the rogue FireSoul that our league was formed to defeat."

Oh boy. This was getting a lot more complex. And a lot scarier. I wanted Victor to be some nobody power-hungry asshat, not some ancient, all powerful evil that inspired the formation of a magical Justice League.

I glanced at Del and Nix. Their queasy expressions showed they were thinking the same.

"So he's been alive for centuries," I said.

"Yes. When he kidnapped you eleven years ago, we staged a rescue attempt," Alton said.

"Eleven years ago was the battle that decimated your numbers," I said.

"It was the same battle. We failed to save you. Your parents and many others died in that fight."

"All to save me?" Horror welled in my chest, pushing on my ribs.

"And them." Alton indicated Del and Nix. "We didn't know who they were, but we assumed that if Victor Orriodor had you, he might have the other members of the Triumvirate. We had waited for you for thousands of years. We couldn't let you die."

Then they had died trying to save the Triumvirate, not me, for whatever great task we were prophesied to accomplish. That was a bit less massively guilt-inducing.

"Thank you to all who fought to save us," I said through a tight throat. How many people had lost their lives trying to free us? It was awful.

"So, what the heck are we supposed to do that's so important?" Del demanded.

"We believe that one task may be to defeat Victor Orriodor," Alton said. "We will give you what help and information we can."

"To get my power back," I said. "I only have a few days before I'm prophesied to meet Victor Orriodor. If I don't have my power by then..." The hourglass was flowing, and my death was at the end.

"You have time," Castille said. "Though the time for talking is done. We will show you what you need to know."

CHAPTER EIGHT

"To defeat your enemy, you must understand him," Corin said.

"All right, Master Splinter," I said.

Corin grinned. "Teenage Mutant Ninja Turtles?"

I shrugged. "It's a pretty high compliment to be compared to a Ninja Rat. He was very wise."

"Fair enough," she said. "I'll take it."

We had been fed a quick lunch in one of the medieval-looking kitchens and were now standing in the courtyard with Alton and Corin.

"If you are ready, I'll take you to see a moment in Victor Orriodor's past," Corin said.

"She's an Illusory," Alton said.

"Wow," I said. I'd love to bring her on some of my temple-raiding jobs. An Illusory could bring the past back to life, replaying events so that present-day people could see them. Illusories were incredibly rare, but I was fascinated by their power.

"Ready?" Corin asked.

She'd replaced her paint-splattered t-shirt with the same red leather armor that Alton wore and had two wicked swords crossed over her back in an X-shaped sheath. With her short blond hair, dark eyes, and firm jaw, she looked like a total badass.

"Yeah." I didn't know where we were headed, but I wanted whatever answers were on the other end.

She drew a small black stone from her pocket. A transport charm.

"Do you have any more?" I asked.

"A small stockpile, though they've recently become harder to come by." She grimaced. "The supply is almost completely cut off. Any wizard we've gone to in the past month no longer has them. All sold."

I frowned and nodded. "Victor Orriodor. We think he's stockpiling. We've had the same trouble finding them."

"He improves his ability to pop out of the air and attack his enemies while cutting off their easy escape," Nix said.

"Bastard," Del muttered.

"That's the truth." Corin's eyes glinted hard.

I wondered if she'd lost anyone in the battle to save us eleven years ago.

"Ready?" she asked.

"Yes," Del said for all of us.

Corin threw the stone to the ground in front of us. It exploded into a glittery gray cloud, and we walked in.

I stepped out on the other side into a massive old-growth forest. The sun was low in the sky, close enough to the horizon that it was probably late afternoon. The forest looked and smelled a lot like the one outside of Aidan's childhood home, not far from the lands of the Alpha Council headquarters at Glencarrough.

"Are we in Scotland?" I asked, thinking of the hovel where Aidan had spent much of his youth.

"Yes," Corin said. "Though this area hasn't been inhabited for hundreds of years."

She pointed to a low stone wall that was only about two feet tall. I walked to it, realizing that it was the footprint of a small home. All that remained were the broken down walls. Corin went to another small stone wall footprint and pointed to it. It was only about ten feet away from the main house and had probably been an outbuilding.

"Where are we?" I asked.

Corin gestured for me to join her near the footprint of the outbuilding. "Come here and I'll show you."

Nix, Del, and I went to her side. She waved her hand toward the old house, and her magic rose on the air. It shivered against my skin like lapping waves.

A moment later, the walls of the house appeared, though they shimmered with a slight transparency. It was a small place, with a thatched roof and only a few tiny windows. Very old, from the looks of it.

The distant beat of horse hooves rumbled the ground. I looked around, trying to find them, but saw only trees. They were still a ways off, though coming fast.

"Can they see us?" I whispered to Corin.

She shook her head.

A woman came out of the house, her apron dusted with flour. Her dress was a drab brown and some kind of old style. Medieval, maybe. Or a bit later. She scanned the forest, her expression terrified.

"It's them, Felix! Argus, come here!" She ran back into the house, but appeared a moment later, towing a small boy by his arm.

He had messy brown hair and looked to be about twelve years old.

"Leave off, Mum!"

"This is what I've been telling you about." Her voice was frantic as she towed him toward us and the outbuilding. "They are coming. You *must* obey me."

Hurriedly, she yanked open the door to the outbuilding and pulled Argus inside. I peered around the door to see in.

She kicked away some straw to reveal a door in the floor.

"I'm not getting in there!" Argus said.

"You will! This is why we've been hiding, Argus. They've found us. You must hide."

"No!" He started to cry, tears spilling down his cheeks.

The woman dropped to her knees and hugged him. "I love you, Argus. But you must hide. Do not come out for anything." She shook him lightly. "Do you hear me? For anything. Wait until all is quiet. Come out, but continue to hide. Forever."

He shook his head frantically. "No! Hide with me."

"I cannot."

A man appeared at my side. I jumped, though he was also a semi-transparent apparition.

"Do as your mother says, son." His dark eyes were weary. Defeated. "It is the only way."

The boy threw himself at his father and hugged him. The sound of hoof beats grew louder.

The man squeezed him as the woman opened the hatch. Argus struggled as his father picked him up and lowered him into the hole.

"Stay," he commanded. "No matter what you hear, stay. Tell no one what you are."

"No!" Argus looked up, his face tearstained.

"Hurry!" his mother said to the man. She looked at Argus. "I love you."

The man lowered the hatch and covered it with straw. The hoof beats were nearly here. My heart thundered as I listened for whatever was coming.

The man and woman hurried away from the outbuilding.

"They have no reason to suspect us," the woman whispered. "We've done nothing wrong. They must let us go."

"You know they don't need proof of what we are. Or proof of wrongdoing." The man leaned over and pulled the woman to him, then pressed a hard kiss to her forehead. "I love you, Lily Crane."

She squeezed him, blinking back tears, and they hurried toward their house.

Just as they were re-entering, a dozen mounted men arrived in the small clearing. They wore old style armor and had full beards, and they formed a circle around Felix and Lily and the house.

"Felix and Lily Crane?" the biggest man demanded.

"We are not them," the man said.

"We have reports that two FireSouls have been living on this land. We have orders to locate them and treat them appropriately," he said.

Felix opened his mouth as if he were going to speak, but he raised a hand and threw a massive fireball at the leader. Magic rose in the air, many signatures at once. Scents, sounds, feelings.

Lily's body glowed as smoke rose up from the forest floor, obscuring her and Felix. The horses stomped their hooves as their riders leapt off.

They stalked toward the gray cloud that hid Lily and Felix. Balls of flame and smoke burst from the cloud, heading straight for the advancing attackers.

A burst of burning smoke landed right in front of us, singeing my clothes. I stumbled back and coughed.

"Is that supposed to happen?" I asked. If they couldn't see us, should we be able to feel the smoke blast?

"No!" Corin waved her hand so that the vision of the past disappeared. The smoke cloud, cottage, and Shifters disappeared.

On the other side of the clearing, only a dozen yards away, stood four shadow demons.

"What the hell?" I drew my daggers from my thigh sheaths.

Before I could fling Righty, something bowled into me from behind. I crashed to the ground, skidding on leaves and roots that scratched my skin. My head rang from the force of the blow, and my chest ached. My shirt was singed and my skin burned, but it was the ache in my sides that made me wheeze. The blast was strong enough to crack ribs. I ignored the pain and scrambled to my feet.

We were back in the real world and were surrounded by shadow demons. Del yanked her short sword out of its scabbard and turned into a phantom while Corin pulled her two swords off her back and threw herself at a pair of nearby shadow demons. Nix conjured a bow and arrow, knelt, and fired straight into a demon's throat. The arrow plowed through and sunk into a tree behind him.

I flung Righty, piercing the heart of a nearby demon. He grunted as he dropped heavily to his knees, then keeled over. Demons fell to our blades as we dodged their blasts of smoke.

When one of them got the drop on Nix, bowling her over with smoke and then leaping on top of her with his dagger raised, I kicked him off, then stabbed him in the neck. Warm blood sprayed me in the face and I gagged, spitting out the disgusting stuff.

I was a pro. I should remember to keep my mouth closed when I stabbed necks. I grabbed my dagger and rolled off him.

"Thanks." Nix panted as she scrambled up. "Looks like five down, two to go."

Corin drew both blades across the neck of a nearby demon, grinning in victory. His head toppled to the ground. Behind her, Del went corporeal long enough to stab a demon through the back. She twisted the blade, pulled it free, then kicked the demon in the back so that he crashed onto his face.

"Check them for transport charms," I said.

Quickly, we rummaged through their pockets.

"Found one!" Nix raised it high, her bare arm showing the distinctive red burn mark of the shadow demon's smoke.

"Me too." Corin stood.

"I'm empty." Del limped toward me, her hand to her side.

"You okay?" I asked as I peered down at my charred shirt. I was still decent, but barely.

"Yeah, just got blasted while I was corporeal. Cracked rib, maybe."

I knew the feeling. My own ribs were aching, a sharp pain coming from the lower left. I breathed shallowly so as not to disturb it as I patted down the last demon, disappointed to find no charms. We were lucky to have found two, considering.

"Let's get out of here," Corin said. "I don't know how they showed up, but I don't want to meet any more."

"Victor Orriodor has a seer hunting me," I said. "Sometimes they get lucky and see through my concealment charm."

"Shitty concealment charm," Corin said.

"Didn't used to be." I joined her under a big tree, Nix and Del at my side. Del and I had our arms wrapped around our middles, trying to lessen the pain of our cracked ribs. Nix blew on her burned arm, though from the grimace on her face, it wasn't doing much good.

Corin tossed the stone to the ground. When the glittery gray cloud poofed up, we walked into it.

Normally I'd hate to waste a transport charm when Del could take us, but if Corin was willing to use her charm, we'd let her. Then Del could save her power for an emergency.

We stepped out on the other side, in the FireSoul Compound. The sun was still shining and the birds still chirping.

"Did we see what we needed to back there?" I asked.

"I'm sure you can guess what happened," Corin said.

"They killed Felix and Lily for being FireSouls."

"Did they find Argus?" Nix asked.

"No. Though he came out to find his parents dead."

I could hardly imagine how horrible that would have been. The poor kid would be scarred for life.

"Why did you show us this?" I asked.

"Because that boy no longer goes by the name Argus. He is Victor Orriodor."

CHAPTER NINE

"Right. Of course," I said. Figured. "So we just witnessed his Super Villain origin story?"

Corin nodded. "Pretty much."

"Makes me almost feel bad for the guy," Nix said.

"Bad for the kid, maybe. Victor Orriodor is no longer that boy," Del said.

"That's for sure." I fiddled with the holstered dagger at my thigh. "So what happened after that?"

"Considering that you're currently a magnet for shadow demons, it's unsafe to bring you there to see for yourself. I don't fancy another fight. But we can go to the library, and the historian will tell you."

"And then you'll tell me how to get my power back?" I asked. I wanted to learn Victor Orriodor's past—Corin was right, understanding him would help me defeat him—but all the magic here at the FireSoul compound was like a blade to my heart. I felt the loss of mine even more keenly.

"Yes," Corin said. "At least, as much as we know. Which I doubt is as much as you want to know."

Damn. "Let's get started, then."

"I'll take you to the infirmary first. Get those wounds looked at." She indicated my charred t-shirt currently flaking away from my chest. "Maybe get you a fresh shirt so your striptease doesn't go all the way."

I grinned and wanted to argue, that we should get a move on with the information, but she was right. If I was ambushed again, it'd be hard to fight with cracked ribs. And I did need a fresh shirt.

We made our way across the courtyard and into a small round building. Inside, everything was white and bright, from the walls to the four narrow beds. Even the healer was a pale man with white-gold hair, as if he, too, had been scrubbed clean.

Boris, as I learned he was called, healed us all quickly with little more than a touch. Aidan had a bit of the same healing ability, but Boris was the real deal.

"Thank you," I said as we left.

He inclined his head, in keeping with his earlier silence.

I felt immensely better as Corin handed me a fresh shirt and then led us into the biggest building I'd seen yet. The massive wooden doors gave way to a huge oval-shaped room. Within was the largest, most fantastic library I'd ever seen. Bookshelves climbed to the ceiling three stories overhead with seven spiral staircases leading to balconies that provided access to the books. The middle of the room was dotted with round tower-shaped bookcases that extended two stories up. Chairs and tables were scattered in between.

"This way." Corin led the way between the towers.

In the middle of the room, a young woman sat at one of the tables. She had pale green hair and pointed ears. A fae or pixie of some kind. Though she looked young, she had a timeless quality about her. Fae lived a long time. I'd put money on her being as old as the building.

"Flora?" Corin said. "We're here to ask you some questions."

Flora looked up at us, blinking wide green eyes. They were slightly blank, as if she'd been in another world inside her head. Even when she looked at us, they didn't focus.

"Yes?" Her voice was vague somehow, as if she were only partially here.

Yeah, she made an appropriate historian for a place like this.

"Sit." Corin gestured to us and the chairs across from Flora.

We sat on the hard wooden surfaces. Flora had turned back to reading her book.

"We don't like to have to ask Flora unless we must," Corin murmured. "She prefers to be left alone. But with the demons hunting you… This is better. I don't know the whole story or I would tell you."

"Flora?" Corin asked.

Flora looked up, eyes slightly blank. "Yes?"

"Could you tell us about Victor Orriodor's history with the League of FireSouls?"

Flora sat back in her chair and gazed into the distance. Her voice sounded far away when she spoke. "At that time, he was called Argus. Five hundred years ago, before we became the League of FireSouls, there was Callum McCord."

Behind Flora, the air shimmered. Her magic floated on the air, the scent of old books and the sound of rustling pages flowing with it. A hazy apparition of a man appeared. He was massive and heavily bearded, his body draped in an old-style cloak.

He must be Callum McCord, and Flora had a crazy ability to project the past. It was different than Corin's gift. Callum was much less substantial, and he was brought to life by nothing more than Flora's words.

"Callum was a FireSoul," Flora said. "But he was also a leader. During his time, it was nearly impossible to live alone. Farming, trading, working, and living—it was all done as a group. This made it difficult for FireSouls to hide from those who persecuted them."

Which was everyone—just like today.

"Callum found FireSouls and offered them a place on his land. He lived in a remote part of Ireland. A peninsula that juts into the sea. There, the FireSouls could live as normal people, dividing the labor as others did, and living more than a scrabbling existence."

Behind her appeared a hazy apparition of a group of people sitting around a rustic dining table. All ages, all clearly coming together after a hard day's work.

"One day, the man who would become Victor Orriodor appeared on their land. He was a FireSoul as well, but he did not seek asylum. He sought vengeance."

Behind Flora, an enraged man appeared. Though her apparition emitted no sound, he was clearly ranting and raving, his hands gesturing wildly. He looked little like the boy I had seen earlier and more like the man I knew today, though he was still young.

"He thought they would help him obtain vengeance for the death of his parents," Flora continued. "They hid out on this remote bit of land because they were persecuted. Attack the persecutors, he said, and be able to live like normal people."

Except that the persecutors were everybody. The Order of the Magica and the Alpha Council may have enforced the laws that FireSouls were scum, but the regular folk propped up that belief with their fear and distrust.

"Of course, he was wrong," Flora said.

Behind her, the people at the table shook their heads, rising to their feet and physically evicting Argus when he wouldn't relent.

"When Argus couldn't find the help he needed, he turned to taking it," Flora said. "He used his FireSoul power in a way that most would never dream. He became what everyone feared, stealing dozens of powers."

And killing everyone he took them from.

"It drove him slightly mad," Flora said. "But in a calm, cold way."

Behind her, Argus appeared, looking older and wearier than before, but with a stern determination in his eyes and a cunning intelligence. I shivered.

"Callum McCord knew that something had to be done," Flora said. "Argus was responsible for many Magica and Shifter deaths, but worse, from Callum's perspective, was that Argus fueled the tide of suspicion and hatred for FireSouls. He was everything that they feared, and as a result, the Alpha Council and Order of the Magica cracked down on FireSouls even harder. Callum's settlement was at risk if he didn't do something."

An image of the FireSoul compound formed behind her.

"So he formed this place and began the battle against Argus, attempting to foil Argus's goals." Her gaze focused on me. It appeared that story time was over, and I was meant to engage.

"Which were what?" I asked.

"Vengeance."

"Against who?"

"Whoever persecuted him. But as you saw in Corin's projection, we do not know who they were. Or what Argus's end goal was."

"Why hasn't he accomplished it yet? It's been hundreds of years."

"Callum successfully stopped him. For a time. They put him into a magical stupor meant to last forever. He was too powerful to kill, but they could entomb him. For hundreds of years, he has been asleep." Flora looked at Corin. "You may finish, as this was within your time."

Corin nodded. "He woke twenty years ago. We don't know how, but he did. I was very young then, and my parents part of the League. He took the name Victor

Orriodor. We think it was to hide his origin from us. But we discovered it and have been attempting to stop him ever since."

"Stop him from what?" I asked.

"His vengeance. Though I fear his goal is even greater. He knew enough to kidnap the Triumvirate." She gestured to the three of us. "It can't be coincidence. Though we don't know what he wants with you."

"Can't be good," Del muttered.

"Nope." I blew out a breath. So, this wasn't great.

Somehow, knowing about his past made him that much more real and much more terrifying. And he was already plenty terrifying to begin with. Not to mention that he'd killed my parents. Whether it had been his hand or another, they had died attempting to rescue us from him.

"This shit just got real," Nix muttered.

"No kidding."

"How do we stop him?" Del asked.

"No idea," Corin said. "After our numbers were decimated trying to save you from his compound, we haven't had the manpower or the skills to find out. Your arrival here marks a turning point."

Talk about pressure. "And my power? Do you know how I can get it back? Or what my root power was?"

"We know neither," Corin said. "We believe that your root power is something no one's ever seen. But it's quite a personal thing. Your parents never said—if they even knew. But we can point you in the right direction to find answers, so that perhaps you can find out for yourself."

"Then which direction do I go?"

"I will get it." Flora rose and moved gracefully toward the corner of the library. Her movements were as eerily calm as her eyes, almost as if she were half-spirit of some kind.

She returned with a rolled up scroll. The paper was yellowed at the edges, the wooden dowel at either end a simple stick rather than the ornately carved ones seen on many scrolls.

Corin moved aside some books to clear a space on the table, and Flora unrolled the scroll, pressing it flat against the wood.

Corin held it open while Flora pointed. "You need to go there."

It was a map—an old one, from the looks of it. The squiggles and lines made no sense to me, though. "Where?"

"The passage tomb where the seer had her vision. You should be able to find answers there."

I sure hoped so. I didn't know if finding out about my root power would help me get rid of the Nullifier's awful power, but it was the only direction I had to go, so that was where I was headed.

We arrived at the Black Fort at sunset. The blazing orange ball was setting behind the cliffs to the west, shining a hazy orange light across the small field of wildflowers that surrounded the statues. The stone wall of the fort rose high, blocking us from the rest of the island. Protecting us.

"Cass!" Aidan loped across the grass toward me and scooped me up in his arms, hugging me tight.

"Oof." He was strong as a freaking bear. "Whoa there, big guy. I'm all right."

He pulled back, his brow quirked. "I know. You're too tough to kill. But I'm glad to see you whole all the same."

I grinned and pulled back. I may not have gotten all the answers I'd wanted, but I was farther along than I had been. And the info about Victor Orriodor might come in handy somehow.

Claire approached, her sunglasses propped on her dark hair. "Success?"

"Sort of. We've got another place to go."

"Good," Connor said. "I've got a hankering to see the world."

"You sure you don't need to get back to P & P?" I asked.

He scowled. "Don't get me wrong. P & P is my baby, but you need us more than the shop right now."

"Thanks." Warmth filled me. They'd proven again and again that they had my back, but every time felt pretty amazing.

"And I'm sorry to say we won't exactly be seeing the world." Del raised the scroll. "These are our directions, and it looks like we're headed south."

Aidan reached for the scroll, and Del handed it over. He unrolled it and frowned at the map, then flipped it over. Understanding filled his eyes.

"This is near my home," he said. "Only about thirty minutes east."

"Ever been there?" I asked. If I'd lived near a passage tomb, I'd definitely have gone exploring.

"No. It's protected by powerful charms."

"Good thing we've got those penatrist charms then," I said.

"Good thing, indeed." He glanced over his shoulder at the setting sun. It'd disappeared behind the cliffs, headed for the sea. "It'll be dark soon. Let's get out of here. We can take my plane. Rest up at my place, then head to the passage tomb in the morning."

I nodded. As much as I wanted to head straight to the tomb, he was right. The tomb had been built by supernaturals. Ancient sites like that were often booby-trapped. Heading into one at night, exhausted, was a surefire way to end up dead.

I took one last glance at the statues that stood silently guarding the portal, vowing to return to see if the apparition of my mother would reappear, then followed my friends across the small field.

We climbed over the rock wall, and by the time we dropped down on the other side, it was nearly dark. The ground was uneven, the slabs of stone making our passage slow.

Aidan pulled out his phone and made a call, speaking in Irish and requesting that the pony traps come to the end of the lane to pick us up.

He said goodbye and lowered his phone. "They'll be here in twenty."

"Thanks," I said.

We made quick work of getting our bags from the house. Unlike at the Black Fort, I didn't look back. I'd return here one day, once all of this was settled, and figure out how I felt about this place. For now, it was too difficult to think of.

Fergus and his friend met us at the end of the lane with the same two pony traps we'd taken to get here. They took us back to the airstrip, their clip-clopping hooves creating a soothing rhythm. The pub we'd passed last night was once again rocking with the sound of trad music. Though there was a lot to talk about, I didn't want to do it in front of the drivers, so I listened to the unique sound of our journey.

My phone buzzed with a text, and I pulled it out of my pocket. Aerdeca's name popped up, along with a message that they hadn't yet found anything about Victor being involved with the Order of the Magica. Whatever he was doing with them, it seemed to be on the down-low. It might not even be in any kind of official capacity. Which made sense, because I might hate the Order, but they wouldn't knowingly ally with someone as evil as him.

"Here we are," the trap driver said when we pulled up in front of the plane.

Only on an island as tiny as this one would a horse drawn carriage be allowed onto a runway. True, we were the only people out here, but still.

"Thanks, Fergus," I said as Aidan paid the driver.

"My pleasure." He handed Aidan a large paper bag.

Aidan took it and turned to me. I nodded inquiringly at the bag.

"Dinner."

I grinned. "You are the best, you know that?"

"I know how you like to eat."

I draped an arm over his shoulders, having to reach up high to do so. "Feeding me is truly one of the finest qualities a man can have."

"I aim to be the finest you ever met."

I grinned. "I'm a lucky girl."

Aidan talked to the pilot while we climbed on board and settled into the plush seats.

"For magic's sake," Claire said. "You really caught a big fish, Cass."

I glanced around at the opulent plane. "Yeah. It's pretty ridiculous, really."

"Yep," Connor said as he ambled into the small kitchen and peered into the fridge. "But I'm going to take advantage of our new high-rolling connections."

He pulled a soda out and tossed it to me. I snagged it out of the air, fumbling it briefly before I got a good grip. Quick as a professional bartender—which he technically was—he grabbed more drinks and tossed them to Claire, Del, and Nix.

It was good to have Connor and Claire here. They kept things feeling a bit more normal when Nix, Del, and I might have gotten bogged down in the enormity of all this.

I popped my soda and took a swig, then sat on the couch that spread along the wall near the back. "So, let's chat."

Aidan entered the plane. "Eat first."

He dug into a big paper bag and pulled out sandwiches wrapped in more paper. He passed them around, and I took mine gratefully. My stomach grumbled as I unwrapped the bundle and revealed a thick ham sandwich.

I took a huge bite, delighted by the taste of sharp cheddar and some kind of sweet onion stuff.

"These Irish know how to make a sandwich," Connor said.

I had to agree. It was no beef and potato pasty like Connor made, but it was damned good. I polished it off so fast that I wasn't sure if I breathed or not.

I swallowed the last bite, comfortably sated, and said, "So, we learned a bit about Victor Orriodor."

I told the story we'd learned, trying not to leave anything out.

When I'd finished, Claire said, "He's still a bastard. Loads of people have effed-up childhoods and don't turn into power-hungry sociopaths."

Her loyalty warmed me.

"So, we know that Victor is after the Triumvirate," Connor said. "Which is you guys."

"Fancy title, by the way," Claire said.

"Thanks. Just wish I knew what we're supposed to do."

"We'll figure it out," Del said.

"It's all tied up in Victor Orriodor, so if we figure him out, I bet we'll figure us out," Nix said.

We talked about what we knew. Victor was out for vengeance, he was somehow involved with the Order of the Magica—which was probably the scariest thing of all—and he'd collected a whole bunch of things that were meant to aid him in his goals.

"So, Victor is like a magpie collecting things to help his end goal." Nix held up her hand and began to tick items off. "Scroll of Truths to find FireSouls, Chalice of Youth for immortality, HeartStone of Glencarrough to protect something of value, and the Celtic cauldron with the massive dampening charm."

"That's quite an arsenal," Del said.

"Don't forget he's bought out pretty much every transportation charm in the world," Aidan said. "It's going to become a lot harder for people to travel quickly in the future, especially since they'll use up their charms before they realize there's a shortage."

"And we've got two," I said, wishing one of us had found the transportation charm that Corin had found. "And two penatrist charms."

"And any potion we want, courtesy of Connor," Claire said.

"Right," Del said. "That's not bad. A pretty good arsenal of our own."

"So, Victor wants vengeance on someone," I said. "And to capture us. We want vengeance on Victor."

"And he wants us," Nix said. "The Triumvirate."

"Right. The Triumvirate." Whatever that really was, it was important. Almost two dozen members of the League of FireSouls had died trying to save us because we were the prophesied Triumvirate. My parents had died trying to save us.

"Do you think that's why we managed to escape Victor's dungeon when we were kids?" I asked, thinking back to our desperate race from his house. "There was almost no one in the house when we ran for it. No guards other than the one I killed. Alton said that the League of FireSouls lost most of their force when they fought to free us. They probably took down as many of Victor's demons, and he hadn't yet replaced them."

"So they cleared the way," Del said.

"Even if they didn't realize it." Nix's eyes glimmered with tears.

My parents saved us, even if they hadn't lived to break us out of the cell themselves. I'd been so close to seeing them.

I slouched back against my seat, suddenly exhausted. Tears threatened, but I forced them back. Now wasn't the time for weakness or weeping.

I thought of my parents, of the people I'd seen in the visions. They wouldn't cry now. They'd fight. Like I would fight.

Up to this point, it'd been a fight for survival. To escape Victor and never be found. Now, it was a fight for vengeance. And to stop whatever awful thing he had planned.

CHAPTER TEN

A shower in Aidan's massive, magical bathroom hit the spot. It was hard not to enjoy a shower with eight shower heads.

We'd arrived at his place thirty minutes ago, and everyone was settled into one of the many bedrooms. The house was protected by enchantments, but that didn't mean that Victor Orriodor's demons couldn't break in anyway. We thought we had their only penatrist charms, but we could be wrong. All they needed was one in order to send in an assassin.

But we'd be ready for them. Aidan had hired guards standing outside every room.

I scrubbed my hair dry and pulled on one of Aidan's giant t-shirts, then made my way out into the bedroom. It felt almost natural by now to be sharing a room with him.

Aidan looked up from the bed where he was sitting with his back propped against the headboard. "Feeling better?"

"Mostly."

He lifted a plate from the bedside table. "How about some cookies? Iona made some earlier today."

The scent of chocolate chips and the memory of his Irish housekeeper's amazing cooking made my mouth water.

"Thanks. You're the best." I took a cookie off the plate and bit in.

"Anytime. Feeding you is part of the gig."

"What gig?"

"Being your better half."

I grinned and would have punched him if I hadn't been preoccupied by the cookie. "So, that's it, then? We're a thing? Like, officially?"

We'd never actually said the words, and though I knew it was probably true because we'd had some pretty intense moments, I wanted to hear him say it. Maybe because everything else in my life was so uncertain, or maybe because I just wanted to hear it.

"Hope that's not news to you."

I shook my head. "Nah. Just wanted you to say it first."

"Happy to be of service."

"So, like, do I call you my boyfriend?" Seemed so juvenile for a guy like him.

He shrugged. "Sure, why not?"

I should have expected that Aidan was comfortable enough in his masculinity not to give a damn what I called him.

"Right, okay." I grinned. "I can do that."

I polished off the cookie and climbed into bed next to him, propping myself against the luxurious padded headboard. Aidan's lifestyle was one I could get used to.

"By the way, I got a message from my assistant," Aidan said. "The Order of the Magica has sent their thanks for your help with defeating the portal, but they're no longer planning to meet with you to thank you."

"Really?" Hope flared in my chest. Finally, something was going right.

"Yes. After you pulled the fire alarm at the Nullifier's memorial, it took them a while to get everything sorted and everyone back in place. They held the memorial, but when we weren't there afterward to meet with them, they assumed we'd left because of the alarm. They don't want to reschedule, so they sent flowers instead."

"Flowers? That's weird. Do you think Victor Orriodor had anything to do with it?"

"Possibly. But flowers the usual cheap and easy thank you for a job well done, so it could just be normal."

I laughed. "I'm being paranoid. And I guess they only kind of appreciated my efforts. But I'll take it as long as Orriodor had nothing to do with it. It's way better than having to meet them."

Aidan grinned as he climbed off the bed. "I thought you'd like to hear that. I'm going to take a shower." But he didn't walk into the bedroom. Instead, he went to the dresser and removed something from the duffle bag he'd set on top when we'd arrived.

"No shower?" I asked.

"I will, but I thought maybe you'd want this before I went." He handed me a picture frame.

I looked down at it. My parents smiled out from the photo. He must have taken it from the house. My throat tightened, but I managed to blink back tears long enough to look at him and say, "Thanks."

He nodded and leaned down to kiss me, then went to the shower.

I listened to the water run as I looked at the photo of my parents. My only two memories of my parents filled my head. And they weren't even real memories. My mother had been an apparition, and I'd witnessed my father and my younger self. I hadn't actually remembered living any moments with them.

My eyes smarted and I blinked rapidly.

"Hey, you okay?" Aidan's voice pulled me from my thoughts.

He was out of the shower already? How long had I been here moping? I scrubbed a hand over my eyes. "Yeah, yeah. I'm fine."

He wore only a pair of tight black boxer briefs and his hair was still wet. My gaze traveled over the cut muscles and the ridges and valleys that were hard to look away from, no matter how bummed I was.

"You don't look fine," he said.

"I'm not handling this well. My parents, the nullifying power. I'm off my game."

"Yeah, of course. You're dealing with some heavy stuff."

"Sure, but I'm not usually such an emotional wimp. There's a lot riding on this, and I'm being so lame about it. My parents were so tough. Nix and Del are so tough. And I've spent more time crying in the last week than I have in my whole freaking life."

"You don't have to be stone, Cass." Aidan sat next to me on the bed and pulled me against his side. "You are only human."

"No, I'm Magica. A strong freaking Magica who is also a giant freaking wimp."

He huffed a short laugh. "It's an expression."

"I know."

"You are tough. And strong. So what if you've been crying lately? Some people just have faces that leak. I once knew a guy who'd cry when he got mad. Angry as fuck, wailing punches, and the stress would make his eyes leak."

I laughed. "You did not."

"I did. On my honor. Crying doesn't make you weak. Lying down and not fighting makes you weak. Who cares if your eyes become fountains when you think about your dead parents or your lost magic?"

"When you put it like that, I guess it doesn't sound so bad." Especially the dead parents part. That part freaking sucked. Who wouldn't cry about that? "But my power. I've been shit about that. I've practiced my nullifying power, but I've gotten nowhere."

"You're fighting it," Aidan said.

"Course I'm fighting it. It sucks. I wanted to shed it like a snake skin."

"You can't fight it away. Forcing it won't work. But you don't have to be powerless. The Nullifier's talent is powerful. It knocked me out of the sky."

I nodded, remembering the time in Switzerland when the Nullifier had turned up the juice on his power and forced Aidan—the freaking Origin, for magic's sake –to lose his magic and turn from a griffin back into a human. In midair. Two thousand feet above a valley in the Swiss Alps.

"You need to embrace your new power, even if only temporarily," Aidan said. "It's a powerful gift, and you may need it."

"But it's fighting inside me."

"Maybe. Aethelred said it's because your innate magic conflicts with it. But also because you won't let it settle." He pointed to the cold cuff still around my wrist. "You're even wearing a dampening charm. That can't help."

"It doesn't really work." But I'd been unable to take it off because I'd hoped it would start working. I knew it was ridiculous, but I couldn't help it. And sometimes *I* was ridiculous.

"I know you want your magic back, and we'll get it. But until you have it, you need to learn to use what you've got. Embrace the change and learn to work with it."

"You're totally right." I hated hearing it, but he *was* right. "How'd you get to be so smart?"

"Just lucky, I guess."

"So how do I embrace it?"

"Take the cuff off, for one."

I slipped the cuff off, not liking the feeling of removing it.

"You're a fighter, Cass. If you see something you want, you fight your way toward it and force it to work."

"Yeah, and I've been pretty successful."

"You have. But times have changed. For most of your life, you refused your power. You're a Magica. You should have been using your power. Instead, you forced yourself and the world to accommodate your will to live without magic."

"I had to. It's the only way I could hide. I'm not going to stop being a fighter." That was who I was. "I can't."

"I don't think you should. It's one of the things I like about you. But some battles don't help us. You need to stop fighting the Nullifier's magic and start fighting for it. At least until you can get rid of it for good. Using it is the smartest thing."

I nodded, my mind spinning with everything that he'd said. "Give me a sec. I want to try."

He squeezed my shoulder encouragingly as I closed my eyes and focused on the magic—or lack of magic—within me. The familiar emptiness greeted me. My chest felt hollowed out, like someone had gotten in there with an ice-cream scoop and gone to town.

This was normally where I retreated. It was the worst feeling, and I didn't want to revel in it.

But if I wanted to succeed, I had to. I'd faced plenty of miserable shit in my life. What was a little more?

The empty feeling in my chest grew as I tried to pull on the Nullifier's magic. To manipulate it to my will and push it outward. Sending it outward meant letting it expand within me.

I broke out in a cold sweat as I tried to embrace the Nullifier's magic and let it fill my whole body.

"Make a flame," I bit out.

I peeked my eyes open to see Aidan hold his hand out and produce a small flame. It flickered orange in the dim room.

I was gonna squash that little sucker.

My breathing grew shallow as I let the Nullifier's magic flow through me. When it filled me down to my fingers and toes—a feeling I wouldn't be remembering with fondness—I tried to grab hold of it.

My normal magic felt robust and distinct. Lightning crackled and sizzled beneath my skin until I released it. Ice felt cold and brittle. The nullification magic felt like I'd grabbed ahold of a ghost.

But I held on to that ghost, pushing it out of myself and toward Aidan.

The flame in his hand flickered and blew, as if a wind had kicked up in the bedroom, but it didn't die. I sucked in a deep breath and pushed harder on the Nullifier's magic. It swelled in the air, prickling against my skin as it left me and flowed outward.

I felt Aidan wince against my side, then the flame in his palm died out.

"Good job." Aidan's voice was rougher than normal. Pained.

Suddenly I felt like shit. "I'm so sorry! I wanted to practice, but I forgot how bad it would feel for you."

I'd hated it when the Nullifier's magic had influenced me in the past. It felt a hell of a lot like what I was feeling now. I might loathe this misery, but I wouldn't wish it on anyone else. Especially not someone I cared for.

Aidan pressed a kiss to my forehead. "Don't worry about it. I wanted to help."

"You did. That's the first time I really felt how the magic worked. I've used it in the past, but it hasn't been so deliberate. This time, I controlled it."

"And you will in the future," Aidan said. "Until the day you get rid of it for good."

"I hope so." Worry gnawed at my chest. "But it was so difficult. And that was just a tiny bit of magic that I nullified. I don't know if I could do much more than that."

"You'll find a way."

I looked up and met his gray gaze. "Thanks for the support. Means a lot."

The corner of his mouth hitched up in a devastating smile. "Anytime."

He was so handsome it made my brain short circuit. I wasn't the type to lose it over looks—there were so many more important things. Kindness, honor, humor, intelligence. That weird, unexplainable quality that made two people fit together like the only matching puzzle pieces in the world.

The thing was—Aidan had *all* those qualities.

And he was so handsome that my brain didn't quite know how to process it. Not to mention the fact that he was currently shirtless.

I climbed on top of him, straddling his waist, and rested my hands on his heavy shoulders as his big hands came up to grip my hips. His pecs were broad wide, flat slabs of muscle that gave way to the ridges of his abdomen.

I allowed myself one quick look before meeting his gaze. "Now I just have to think of a way to repay you."

"You don't need to repay me." Despite his words, his heated gaze dipped down, running over my body. I was wearing a tent of a shirt, but Aidan seemed to like the hints he got.

Heat flowed through my limbs, gathering in the most interesting places.

"Oh, but I want to." I pressed a kiss to his throat, darting my tongue out to taste his clean skin. The soap-clean Aidan smell of him made my toes curl.

His head fell back against the headboard and he groaned, a low rumble in his throat that sent shivers over my skin. I tightened my thighs around his hips, liking the feel of him beneath me.

I ran my mouth lower, delighting in the smooth skin against my lips. My tongue darted out to taste him and he jerked, his fists tightening against my hips. His strength sent a frisson of excitement through me.

I dragged my tongue lower, toward his abs and the much more enticing destination concealed by the black cotton stretched tightly over his hips.

I glanced up to see his muscles clenched tight and the veins standing out at his throat.

He liked this. A lot.

I darted my tongue out, licking his smooth skin. He groaned and gripped the headboard, his arms straining as he nearly crushed the wood.

"Jesus, Cass." His voice was rough with desire. "Be careful, or I might start thinking you want me."

"What if I do want you? What if I want everything?" And I did. I wanted him so badly my body felt like it was on fire. If he wanted me back had protection, I'd be all over him.

His dark eyes snapped to mine, fire in their depths. "Then I'm inclined to give it to you."

I grinned, then reached a hand to the waistband of his boxers and lowered my mouth to his abs.

"Any special requests?" I murmured against his skin.

"Just you." He reached down and pulled me up, pressing a kiss to my lips. When he pulled away and his and his gaze met mine, I knew I was probably in for the best night of my life.

CHAPTER ELEVEN

I'd been right. It had been the best night of my life. Which was why I hadn't gotten nearly enough sleep last night and this hike across a totally flat field felt like I was going uphill.

Aidan and I had woken after only a few hours of sleep and were now hiking over a field in the wee hours before dawn with my *deirfiúr* and Connor and Claire. The moon was setting over the trees in the distance, shedding a silvery light over the recently-harvested hay.

"Think we're close?" Del asked.

"It's right up ahead." Aidan pointed into the distance.

I squinted through the dark, trying to find the passage tomb we sought.

"That pile of grass?" Del asked.

"That's the one," Aidan said.

"Not very impressive, is it?" Claire asked.

I had to agree with her. It looked like nothing more than a grassy bump in the field, maybe a hundred meters wide.

"Wait 'til you get inside," Aidan said. "That'll be where it gets good."

From what I knew of passage tombs, it was a massive pile of stones with a central passage leading to a collection of rooms built inside. There may have once been a stone wall marking the exterior and possibly even a stone top. But in the thousands of years since it'd been built, grass had grown over the entire thing, concealing the magic within.

The six of us neared it a few minutes later.

"Taller than it looked from back there," Connor said.

"Yeah," Claire added. "Wider too. Not so unimpressive anymore."

"But where's the door?" Del asked.

"Let's look." I started around the side, hoping it would be obvious. I raised my hand, igniting the magic in my lightstone ring so that I could see better. The grass could have completely obscured the door, and that would suck.

"How long since anyone has used this thing?" Nix asked. "And what did they use it for?"

"It was ceremonial, like a temple. And possibly also used for burial," Del, our resident historian, said. "It's probably been abandoned for thousands of years. Passage tombs like these are over five thousand years old."

"Old as the pyramids." Surprise rang in Connor's voice.

"Yep," Del said.

On the other side of the cairn, we hit the jackpot. A massive stone slab was set into the side of the hill, too steep for grass to have grown over it. I held my lightstone ring closer. Beautiful swirled designs had been painstakingly carved into the stone.

"There's the door," I said.

"What's that hole above it?" Nix asked.

I looked up to see a horizontal shaft built into the cairn. Four slabs of stone made a square hole. I looked around, searching for the glow of the rising sun to get my bearings. Behind me, the haze of dawn crept over the horizon.

I hiked my thumb back toward the sun. "Sun rises in that direction, so that hole is meant to let light in during the summer or winter solstice," I said. "Assuming this is like other passage tombs, it would shine down the passageway into the main room."

"Cool," Claire said. "So how do we get in?"

I stepped up to the stone and peered around the edges, running my hands up the sides. But the slab of rock made a seal with the grass on either side. Which meant it made a seal with the stone behind it, effectively blocking the entrance.

"There's no easy way in," I said.

"When humans built cairns like these, they often put a big stone like this at the front," Del said. "Anyone who wanted in would have to climb over it."

"So the supernaturals made their cairn even harder to enter," Connor said. "Of course."

I laid my palms on the stone, hoping to feel the magic and get an idea for what we had to do to get inside. All I could feel was the dull hum of the protective spell, which prickled against my skin like gnat bites.

I withdrew my hand and stepped back.

"I can try transporting in." Del looked at me. "Can I borrow your lightstone ring?"

I pulled it off and handed it to her.

She shoved it on. "Can someone give me a boost so I can peek through the light shaft up there? I don't want to transport straight into rock."

Aidan crouched by the stone and cupped his hands. Del put her foot in his hands, and he lifted her up. She peered into the light shaft, sticking her arm through so that my ring could light up the interior.

"Looks like a narrow passage," she said. "You can let me down."

Aidan lowered her.

"See you in a sec." She closed her eyes, and I smelled the clean laundry smell of her magic.

But nothing happened.

She turned to face us. "Doesn't work."

"Damn."

Her magic swelled again, and her skin faded and turned a glimmering blue. "I'll go see if there's a switch to open it, like in the pyramid."

She glided toward the stone door.

Then bounced off.

"Well, that's weird," she said. "Never had that happen before."

"Okay, right," Nix said. "We have a problem."

"Not yet, we don't." I liked these kinds of riddles. My job was all about getting into places like this.

Del tugged off my lightstone ring and handed it back to me. I put it on and raised it, then stepped up to the stone again and tried to clear my mind, looking for a pattern or a clue.

There had to be a way in, and if the obvious hadn't worked, then it was going to be subtle. I glanced over the carved swirls, looking for a pattern. This place had been built in the time before metal tools. Someone had sat here for hundreds of hours, pecking away with rock against rock. Had they done it for art? Or for a more practical purpose? Or both?

Eventually, my eyes picked out a loose pattern. More like a cluster, as if the swirls were pointing toward the right side of the door. Or flowing away from that side of the door. There was a blank space there that had no carved decoration.

I stepped up close to the blank space, shining my light at an angle across the rock and pressing my face into the stone to look sideways.

My light caught on a little edge of rock, casting a shadow and revealing the clue I'd been seeking.

"A handprint," I murmured. It was such a shallow indention that I hadn't seen it when shining the light directly on it. I'd needed the shadow to see.

"Really?" Del shoved her face close to mine and looked. "Yep. Totally a handprint."

We stepped back.

"Here goes nothing." I pressed my hand to the space where I'd seen the handprint, settling my fingers against the shallow groves.

But nothing was exactly what happened. I waited a second more, but still nothing.

"Okay." I stepped back and looked at the door.

"We're close," Del said. "That's definitely a handprint, and it's definitely the way in."

"We need something more," Aidan said. "We've only got part of the puzzle."

Tomb raiding was kinda fun with a team. Usually I did this stuff on my own—with Nix on the comms charm for backup—but many hands made light work, as someone smarter than me once said. In this case, it was many minds, but I'd take it.

"These places were usually ceremonial," I said, thinking out loud. "People came here to honor the dead, maybe even to bury them. And to honor their gods."

"Gods like sacrifice," Del said.

Her words triggered something in my mind. "That they do."

I pulled Lefty from its sheath and made a narrow slice across my right palm, wincing as the blade bit into my skin. Sharp pain flared as blood welled.

"Smart," Del said.

"You should have told me to do it," Aidan said.

I ignored him, though I appreciated his willingness, and pressed my palm to the handprint, letting my blood soak into the stone.

Magic flared, and the prickling sensation of the protective charm dissipated. The huge stone door shimmered, turning transparent.

"Cool," Connor whispered.

I withdrew my hand. "Yeah, very."

I stepped forward and held out my lightstone ring, peering inside. A long, straight passage led deep into the cairn. It was incredibly narrow, and the walls and low ceiling were built from dry-stacked stone. No mortar, just cleverly placed rocks that properly distributed the weight of thousands of pounds of stone overhead.

I shivered to think of it collapsing on me, but if it had lasted this long, it'd probably keep standing.

"Connor and I will guard the entrance," Claire said. "You go do your thing."

"Thanks." I stepped into the passage, vaguely aware of the fact that Del and Nix followed behind me, and Aidan behind them.

The haunting beauty of this simple place wowed me, even more than the pyramid had. Maybe because my fate had been prophesied here, thousands of years ago.

Was my magic really that ancient? Was I really tapped into something that old? I'd always felt an affinity—love, even—for the ancient sites I'd visited, but this place was something special.

The passage narrowed in places, and I turned sideways to slip though, keeping my daggers at my thighs from scraping against the stone walls. Twice, I had to duck when the ceiling lowered. Aidan was probably having a rough time of it, considering how much bigger he was.

After about thirty yards, the passage ended in a small room. It was only about twelve feet by twelve feet, with three smaller rooms extending off of that. One directly ahead and one on either side. They were accessible only by a hole to crawl through rather than a real doorway and were about half the size of the room we stood in now.

"A cruciform passage tomb," Del said. "The room's laid out so it's shaped like a cross. These were common."

I looked up. The low ceiling of the passage had given way to a high domed ceiling made of stone. Once again, there was no mortar. Just carefully placed stone that overlapped at regular intervals, creating a beautiful ceiling.

There was nothing on the ground in the main room, but when I peeked into the smaller rooms, there were massive stone basins sitting in the middle of each one.

"The ones on the sides hold bones," Del said.

I peered into the room directly opposite the passageway. "This one has offerings."

Bowls, a few golden trinkets, and bone carvings were laid neatly in the stone basins. I retreated and looked into the other rooms at the bones of long-dead people. They weren't laid out like bodies, but rather small clusters, as if the person had been laid here a while after death once all their bones could be gathered into a neat pile.

The walls in each of the small rooms were covered in carvings.

"I don't understand the carvings," I said. "They're just swirls and flowers."

"Nature symbols," Del said. "Makes sense, for a culture so in tune with the land."

But none of them were recognizable. They had been, once. But not to me. I didn't know what I'd expected—a picture book story of my life? One that told the future and how to fix it?

That would have been nice.

Unlikely, but nice.

"See what kind of magic you can feel," I said.

We each chose a room, pressing our hands against the stone and trying to sense any ancient magical signatures that might have been left behind. When I got to the room opposite the passage, I felt a strong thrum of magic.

"There's something weird here," I said. "The magic feels like it's contained, but it's pushing against the boundary. It wants to be set free."

"None of us have that gift," Aidan said.

He was right. The ability to manipulate old or latent magic was a rare one. I stepped back and looked around, trying to get a feel for how this would work if I were a person from this temple's heyday, paying a visit.

There was no guarantee that person would possess the ability to release the magic stored in the stone, or that they would even know someone with that ability. It was likely they wouldn't. I lived in a massive, modern city, and I'd never met someone like that.

"I don't think that's our answer." My gaze traveled around the room, landing on the exit passageway. I couldn't see the outside because it was blocked, but the passage glowed slightly with the golden light of dawn. The sun had risen while we'd been in here.

"Ooooh," I murmured as my gaze darted back to the room that contained the latent magic. It was exactly opposite the entry and light shaft. "The solstice."

Del's gaze darted between the entry and the room with the magic. "Holy shit. You're right."

"Right about what?" Nix said. "I'm going to need some help here."

Del was the history buff. Nix had other skills. This wasn't one of them.

I pointed to the exit. "At the solstice—summer or winter, I'm not sure which—the sun shines through the light shaft, travels up the passage, and hits the wall. It probably ignites the magic."

Nix's brows rose. "Cool." She looked down the passage. "But I can't see the exit from here. Shouldn't I be able to see it if the light will travel uninterrupted?"

Aidan grinned. "The floor slopes up. I thought that was strange. But it's so the light, which enters above the door, can shine right on the wall, which is at the same level."

"Bingo." I knew I liked him.

"But it's not a solstice," Del said. "We're months away from either one."

"We won't have to." Excitement laced Nix's voice. "We'll make our own solstice."

"How?" Del asked.

"Okay, hear me out. Aidan will go outside and use his elemental mage powers to make a fireball the size of a house. Claire's a Fire Mage, so she can help. I'll conjure mirrors. We'll send light down the shaft, and the magic will ignite. Easy peasy."

Whoa, that was good. And yep, Nix had her own talents. Clever problem-solving was one of them. And, holy magic, was I glad I had such a sharp team at my back.

"I like it," Aidan said.

Del nodded. "Definitely worth a try."

"Good one, Nix," I said. "I'll wait here. You guys go do your thing."

They retreated, and Del went with them to help hold the mirrors. When I lost sight of them down the passage, the chamber became eerily silent. I looked around, a chill going over my skin.

It wasn't a bad chill, or a fearful one. Just one of enormity. I stood here with what were very possibly the bones of my ancestors. Five thousand years before I'd been born, someone had prophesied my birth and my gift.

It was huge. It was weird. It was my life.

"Stand against the wall!" Nix's voice drifted down the passage.

I climbed into the small chamber on the left and pressed my back against a side wall so that I wouldn't block the shaft of light.

A few moments later, a sharp beam of warm yellow light stretched across the floor, reaching from the passageway toward the back room.

It was a magical experience, watching something that had been the peak holy experience for a group of people long dead.

The golden light stretched farther, reaching for the back wall, and I could imagine Aidan and Claire casting enormous fireballs, with Nix, Del, and Connor holding up three massive mirrors to strengthen the light and send it this way.

I held my breath as the beam of light reached for the wall. When it finally hit the bottom, it illuminated a carving of concentric circles.

Magic swelled, ancient and powerful. It made the hair on my arms stand up and my breath catch in my chest. The wall glowed as more magic swirled in the air and coalesced into the form of a person.

The figure was featureless and slender, though it seemed to be female.

The seer.

"Hi," I said, then felt quite stupid. But what else was I going to say? *Good morning, Madame Seer?*

Her form became clearer, glowing golden and bright. Her face looked young, no older than me, but she gave the impression of age and wisdom.

"Cassiopeia McFane. Cassiopeia Clereaux." Her voice sounded like the wind and ocean and birds, unlike any human's voice I'd ever heard. And her magic smelled like springtime, flowers and grass and a cool breeze.

"Both work."

"I have been waiting for you." Though she didn't speak English, I understood her.

I grinned. "You didn't exactly make it easy for me to get in and chat."

She smiled. "But you got in all the same."

"Hard to keep me out of a temple I want to get into."

"I imagine so." She turned and looked around the temple. "But this temple is special. You are here amongst your ancestors."

"It's pretty cool." Cool? Who said cool to an ancient seer spirit who was probably also their great grandma one thousand times back? Hang on. *Was* she related to me? "Are you my great grandmother, times a million?"

"I am not. But I am of your family, somewhere down the line."

"Which is why I had to come here for answers?"

"Our magic is old and great. You must come to the source for the answers you seek."

"About my powers. What was my root power? Where did it go when I pushed it toward Del? How do I get it back? How do I get rid of the Nullifier's power?"

"That is a lot of questions." She smiled. "But they are all connected. I have some answers. The rest are at the Black Fort. You will be able to unlock what you seek there with the help of your *deirfiúr*."

"But how?"

"That is for you to find out. I do not know how to unlock the secrets of the Black Fort. It was built after my time." She knelt and picked up a thin ring made of twisted golden wire, then handed it to me. "Take this. It is enchanted to help you focus your magic."

Focusing and using the Nullifier's new power had been one of my problems. I took the ring and put it on, surprised to feel that it fit perfectly on my middle finger. But my magic didn't feel any different.

"It was left here thousands of years ago," she said. "Intended for you."

"Wow." I shivered at the idea of one of my ancestors enchanting the ring and leaving it for me.

"But I can get my power back, right?" I needed an answer to that question more than any other.

"Yes."

My shoulders loosened. As long as that was true, I could face what came at me.

"The Triumvirate will help you with your coming task," she said. "It is the source of your magic and your strength. Rely on them when times are hard."

"What does that mean? What are we supposed to do?"

"A great battle is coming. You three will have a role to play if the light is to succeed."

"Victor Orriodor."

"He is part of it."

"There's more?" Of course there was. And of course she spoke in the usual seer language. All twisty and random. Like how Victor Orriodor's seer had spoken. "A couple weeks ago, another seer spoke about me. He called me 'the Gifted.' Does that have anything to do with my root power?"

She nodded. "It could. Your root power is one of a kind. It is linked to your role in the Triumvirate."

"But I represent *power* in the Triumvirate, which doesn't make a lot of sense."

"Doesn't it? Along with life and death, magic is the other leg of the tripod that supports the world we all know."

Power-fueled magic. "So I have more power than others?"

"Power everlasting. Power eternal."

Everlasting? Like the Energizer Bunny, just going and going and going?

"Am I a magical battery?" I asked.

"I do not know what that is."

Of course not. The most advanced technology she'd known was fire.

"My root power is the ability to never run out of magical energy," I guessed. No wonder Victor Orriodor had tried to steal it all those years ago. *That* was a valuable power. "I could fuel a million spells without growing weak."

"Yes, precisely. Though it would take practice to control that much magic. You would still become physically exhausted by the strain. But with practice—years of it—you could become the most powerful magical force in history."

Whoa.

Whoa, whoa, whoa.

"So where did it go? How do I get it back?"

"It went into Del."

"But she can't feel it inside herself." Had she lost it somehow?

"She cannot access it, though she does have it within her. If you were not linked by the Triumvirate, she may have lost it forever. She was able to save it for you."

"And I can get it back from her?" Hope—real, solid, tangible hope—filled my chest. This was something I could work with.

"Yes. If everything goes well, you can get it back. But you must unlock it within her."

"How?"

"At the Black Fort. That is a sacred place for the Triumvirate. The magic there will help you."

"Okay." My mind raced with the questions I had for her. So many. "But how do I use my magic if I still have the Nullifier's power dampening my own? And what about the great battle you spoke of? How will Del, Nix, and I win?"

"You start by getting your power back. Then you each have a role to play." The golden glow that formed her body flickered. She looked at her hand. "I am running out of time."

"No! You haven't answered my questions."

"I have answered the most important. The one that I have been waiting to answer. And I have given you the ring that has been waiting for you. You have the tools to get your power back. The rest is up to you."

The rest seemed like a lot. "Please stay. What can I do to make you stay? Do you need more light?"

I prayed Aidan and Claire had enough juice left to keep their flame going.

"There is nothing you can do. I must go." She faded, her body becoming a transparent cream color rather than a glimmering gold.

I reached out for her, but it was too late.

She faded away.

Damn. I turned to go, my mind in a daze, then stopped short.

A tribute. I needed to leave a tribute. Wasn't that what my ancestors had done, here in this temple? They'd left the ring for me, but the stone basin in her room was full of gifts. Just because I had the answers I sought didn't mean I shouldn't leave one.

I shrugged out of my jacket—one of my favorites that had cost an arm and a leg—and laid it in the basin.

"Thank you." I touched the basin one last time, feeling connected to her and my past, before turning and walking out.

I shivered as I made my way through the narrow passage. When I reached the exit, I had to shield my eyes against the massive flame Aidan and Claire had created. Huge mirrors were set up behind it, directing the light into the passage.

Not a bad solstice.

"Cass." Aidan's voice sounded relieved.

The flame died suddenly, and Nix, Del, and Connor slowly lowered the mirrors to the ground.

"Did it work?" Del asked.

"Yes." I fingered the ring that I wore on my right hand. I finally fully understood my root power and had an idea about how to get it back. "But we have a long way to go."

CHAPTER TWELVE

I dropped down onto the grass inside the wall at the Black Fort. Aidan landed next to me, followed by Nix, Del, Claire, and Connor. The sun hung low in the sky, ready to set.

We'd gone straight from the passage tomb to Aidan's place, grabbed our stuff, then taken his plane to Inismor. On the way, I'd told them what I'd learned.

"I shouldn't be surprised we're back here," I said.

"This place is important." Nix looked around, thoughtfulness in her gaze. "It makes sense that it'll help us transfer your magic back to you."

Aidan squeezed my shoulder, and I leaned into him.

"I wish I knew what to do." I started across the grass toward the stone circle, my gaze riveted to the statues.

The seer had had faith in my ability to figure this out, but it seemed a lot harder than breaking into a temple. If my mom showed up again with directions, that would be one thing. But I doubted we'd get that lucky.

I stopped in the middle of the stone circle, facing the statues with the other standing stones at my back. "I don't understand how I'm supposed to use my power once I get it back. If I still have the Nullifier's gift, won't it crush it?"

"Or the other way around," Aidan said. "Your own magic could overpower the Nullifier's."

Hope made my heart feel light. "You're right."

"We just need to figure out how I can give your power back to you." Del paced around the statues, eyeing them up and down. She stopped in front of hers, gazing up at it. "I sure do look creepy."

I looked closely at her statue. She was right. The skeletal thinness of her statue gave it an eerie look.

"I think it's symbolic," I said, hoping to make her feel better.

"Yeah, symbolically ugly."

"I won't brag that I get to be Snow White." Nix petted the head of the deer next to her own statue. "Now how to convince these guys to clean my house..."

I grinned as I walked around my statue, but it didn't take long for the grin to fade. There was nothing obvious about it. No lever, no place to lay a tribute, no patterns or inscriptions. Just statues, simply carved and elegant.

Del touched her statue. It glowed brightly with white light, which flowed to Del and lit her from within.

"Holy shit." Nix's wide gaze went from Del to her own statue. She removed her hand from the deer's head where it had been resting and touched her own statue. It glowed with a golden light. Like with Del, it flowed from the statue to Nix, lighting her up from within until she shone like a golden beacon.

The light then traveled over to Del until they were linked by a glowing wire of light. A pair.

"Wow," Del said. "We should have touched these earlier."

I touched my statue. I felt the pulse of magic, but my skin didn't glow like theirs had. No glowing golden wire connected me to them. I stepped back, frustration beating at my chest with tiny fists. "Why won't it work for me?"

"Do you feel a connection to it when you touch it?" Del asked.

"I feel magic, but I don't know if it's a connection."

Del removed her hand from her statue. She stopped glowing and the golden light that connected her to Nix faded. She approached my statue and touched it, then frowned.

"My magic links with the magic in my statue," Del said. "But when I touch yours, I feel like I'm blocked."

"You both have your magic, but I don't have mine. So maybe my statue doesn't recognize me," I said. It sounded weird to say that a statue didn't recognize me, but this was a powerful magical place. Normal rules didn't apply here.

"Only you should be able to access your statue's power," Nix said. "So it's probably protecting itself."

"Oh," I murmured, understanding suddenly hitting me. I had to nullify the protection charm that was on the statue. Then I could make the connection. But could I?

It'd been so difficult to nullify Aidan's flame last night, and this was so much bigger.

I shoved up the sleeve of Aidan's jacket, which he'd loaned me after I'd left mine at the passage tomb, then pulled off the golden cuff and set it on the grass.

The ancient ring that the seer had given me suddenly glowed warm on my finger. I glanced down at it. I felt different. More peaceful or more in control. Maybe both. Like the ring could finally work now that I wasn't wearing the dampening charm, and it was helping to calm the magic fighting within me.

Suddenly, I felt like I could do it. I'd practiced, but the ring from my ancestors would help me.

"You've still been wearing that dampening charm?" Nix asked.

I shrugged. "Yeah. But I'm starting to think some people are right." I glanced at Aidan, who smiled slightly. "It's a safety blanket against my unwillingness to accept change."

"Been watching a lot of Dr. Phil, lately?" Del asked.

"Yeah, yeah. I sounded like a freaking therapist. But I'm finally figuring this stuff out. I may hate the Nullifier's magic, but I need it."

"For what?" Nix asked.

"Whatever magic the statue is using for protection, I'm going to try to nullify it so I can make a connection with it." I thought maybe I could feel it, humming beneath the stone. A slight prickle against my skin. "Then you guys can touch yours and hopefully we'll be connected."

"Then maybe your magic will flow from me to you." Del turned to her statue and touched it. Immediately, she began to glow.

"Good idea," Nix said. As soon as she touched her own statue, she glowed as well. A thin thread of light extended from Del to Nix, linking them.

"Give it a go," Aidan said to me.

I turned to face the statue and rested my hands against it. The magic thrummed against my fingertips, but it didn't flow from the stone into me.

With a deep breath, I closed my eyes and focused on the Nullifier's magic. It was incorporeal, but it was easier to get ahold of now that I was wearing the ring from my ancestors. I envisioned lowering the defenses protecting the statue. It was just like a box holding treasure. All I had to do was get in.

"Is she glowing?"

I heard someone whisper as if from far away, but I kept my focus on trying to nullify the protection charm. I didn't dare open my eyes to see if they were right.

The Nullifier's power flowed through me, strange and empty feeling. I suppressed a shudder as I let it fill me, trying to replicate the practice I'd done with Aidan. This was a much bigger task than nullifying the small flame he'd created, but the ring helped me access the Nullifier's magic.

The ghost of power flitted through me, gaining strength. Once I felt it vibrating through my whole body, I tried to push it outward, toward the statue. Like an oil spill, it needed to coat the magic that I wanted to nullify.

My head spun, but I didn't let up. When my breath grew short from the strain, I pushed harder, trying to force the Nullifier's magic into the statue. I felt like I had one chance at this.

When I opened my eyes, my statue was glowing. I glanced to my right. The thread of light now connected Nix, Del, and I! It glowed brighter and stronger, connecting the three of us and our statues, like a conduit that ran between us all.

A ball of light pushed its way out of Del's chest, flowing into her statue. It traveled across the light wire, toward my statue.

As it neared, a ringing sounded in my ears, growing louder and louder until a blast of power burst from my statue, lighting up the night. It exploded with the force of a sonic boom, throwing me to my back on the grass.

Soul-shaking power flowed through me, lighting me up like a live wire. I vibrated with energy, nearly blind with the shock. Vision hazy, I blinked, struggling to my feet.

When my sight cleared, all I saw was darkness. A sparkle of stars and swirls of light coalesced in the distance, but I no longer stood in the stone circle. My friends were nowhere to be found.

I trembled with power, magic coursing through me like a drug, and I spun, still slightly dazed.

Where was I?

Two figures approached me, both glowing white in the dark.

When they neared, I could make out the distinctive red hair of the woman and the tall, dark-haired figure of the man.

My heart leapt. "Mom. Dad."

"Cass." My mother held out her arms.

Joy surged through me. This time, I could tell she was real. She wasn't a solid figure, but she was more than the apparition that had guided me back at the stone circle.

They stepped forward and hugged me. Comfort like I'd never known flowed through me. I wanted to feel it forever. Their arms were as solid as if they'd been real, but they were semitransparent, like ghosts.

"Am I dead?" I asked.

My mother stepped back and smiled. "No."

"Then where am I?"

"I don't know, exactly," my father said.

"I think this is what we prepared for," my mother said to him.

"What do you mean?"

"When you were born, we knew you were special. *Actually* special. Not just special because you were ours. We moved to Inismor because we thought it would be a good place to raise you. The next day, the statues appeared at the Black Fort."

"We realized you were part of the Triumvirate and knew you might be hunted. So we had the locket created to protect you. We didn't know if someone would try to steal your power, but we suspected it could happen."

"So it protected me when Victor Orriodor tried to take it."

"Yes. Though we didn't expect you to give your power to your friend," my father said.

"I had to do it."

"Yes, you did," my mother said. "It saved your life. And you were able to get it back. The statues connect you with Del and Nix, but they are also a conduit for your magic, making it stronger."

"But you'll have to practice with your gift," my father said. "You have endless power, but you will be unskilled at wielding it. Until you have control, you will be dangerous."

"I wish we'd been able to train you." My mother squeezed my shoulder.

My father draped an arm over her shoulder. "We wouldn't have known how. This was for the best."

"Thank you for saving me from Victor's dungeon when I was a kid," I said.

Pain glinted in my mother's eyes. "We didn't succeed."

"You did." I hugged her. "You made it possible for us to escape. Without you, we never would have made it out of the house."

My mother squeezed me hard, then stepped back and said, "You must go now. Your friends need you."

My heart constricted. "I want to stay with you longer."

"You cannot. You are now at some kind of waypoint, able to talk to us, but your friends are back on Earth. When you lowered the protective charms on the circle and released your magic, you destroyed your concealment charm and all the protections on the Black Fort. He is coming for you."

Victor Orriodor. "Will I see you again?"

"One day," my mother said.

"So the afterlife is real?"

"Where do you think we came from?" my father said.

I grinned, bittersweet joy flooding my chest, and hugged them, never wanting to let go.

Half a second later, I opened my eyes back on earth. I was on my back in the grass, staring up at the stars. I struggled to my feet, my heart fuller than it had been in years.

The world had turned eerie while I was away. Gray mist drifted along the ground. The grass beneath had been singed, almost incinerated.

By me?

My friends all lay on their backs, the gray haze curling around them. I dropped to my knees by Claire, who lay nearest me.

"Wake up!" I shook her shoulder.

She blinked, her gaze confused. "What's happened?"

Around us, figures appeared at the edges of the circle. Each carried a flaming sword that glowed bright in the night, cutting through the gray fog.

"Shit," I whispered.

There were over a dozen, and more kept appearing.

"Get up!" I shouted. "Everyone, wake up!"

I surged to my feet, and Claire struggled upright. The rest of my friends stood slowly, shaking their heads and trying to get their bearings.

They stood not a moment too soon. The demons entered the stone circle, bypassing any protection charms that might have once been there.

The fight broke out in half a second as the demons charged. Everyone jumped into action. A swirl of gray light surrounded Aidan, and a moment later, the massive griffin stood in his place. He roared, then launched himself into the sky and swooped on the demons, crushing their heads in his beak. Blood sprayed.

Claire threw massive fireballs toward one group of demons, her flame lighting up the night. The fire bowled them over, but more followed behind.

Connor threw potion bombs, which exploded on the demons in flashes of color. Demons shrieked as his acid coated their skin. Del became a phantom, her bright blue form stark against the dark night, while Nix conjured her bow and arrow, cutting down demons left and right.

But more appeared for every one we killed.

My daggers could do nothing against this. No matter how fast I threw, I couldn't keep up.

But I had my powers back. Better than that, I had eternal magical energy. I could fuel so many spells that I'd take out armies, masses of soldiers at a time.

My magic vibrated beneath my skin, a massive amount of power that was so different from the emptiness I'd felt while I'd had the Nullifier's gift. Aidan had been right—my own magic had driven out the Nullifier's power.

Joy and strength surged through me as I called upon my magic. There were so many demons that I'd have to use something big. Aidan's Elemental Mage gift would work well.

Using my Mirror Mage powers, I reached out for Aidan's signature, trying to get ahold of his power over flame. There was so much magic in the air that it was hard to find it at first. Finally, I grasped on to the scent of smoke and heat of flame that marked Aidan's gift and crafted a massive fireball.

The flame burned inside my chest, roaring to be released. It thundered within me, stronger than it had ever been. I turned toward a group of demons who were racing toward Claire and hurled my fireball at them.

A jet of flame the size of a city bus hurtled through the air. Worse, a blast of magic exploded from me, like a sonic boom radiating across the grass and throwing everyone to their backs.

I crashed to the ground with everyone else, the wind blown from my lungs. My magic screamed inside me, going haywire. I shook from it as I scrambled up, panting. Chaos surrounded me. Bodies everywhere. Not a single person or demon stood besides myself.

Fear shot like ice through my veins, chilling my bones. My chest ached. Had I killed them all?

What the hell *was* my gift?

I raced toward the nearest body—Aidan. In the blast, he'd turned back into his human form. As I fell to my knees beside him, the scent of rot and decay rolled over the stone circle. Invisible bee stings pricked my skin, and a taste like death coated my tongue.

Terror seemed to freeze my muscles solid, and I had to force myself to look up. My heart froze as my gaze met Victor Orriodor's.

He stood outside the circle, his immaculate suit looking out of place in the blown-apart landscape that I'd created with my magic.

"My, my." His voice was colder than the arctic. "Did you do all this, FireSoul?"

He called me FireSoul, like he had last time we'd spoken at Ephesus. So he still didn't know my real name. Just that I was the FireSoul he sought. Most likely, he didn't care what I called myself.

In front of me, Aidan shifted. Barely.

Not dead.

Relief flowed through me. I had to keep Victor talking while my friends recovered from the mess I'd created. I could try to sonic boom the bastard, but I'd probably just hurt my friends more. Or kill them. They were weakened by my disastrous attempt to use my new strength.

I'd felt a sonic boom before. Victor Orriodor's, in fact. It was one of his gifts. It could crush your organs and kill you, especially if you received multiple hits. That was what'd killed the Nullifier.

But I couldn't control it like Victor could. It was a byproduct of my new strength, not the point of the spell. If I produced one again, I could kill my friends.

Blustering my way through it to buy some time was the only thing I could think to do. "What, Victor? You here to kill me?"

"Kill you?" Incredulity colored his voice. "Why on earth would I do that?"

"Oh, I don't know. After your goons tried to drown me in the Pool of Memory, I sort of figured that was your goal."

He shook his head, disappointment clear on his face. "No. That wasn't supposed to happen. They were trying to pull you from the pool. But tricky thing, that Pool of Memory. It wouldn't let you go."

"So they decided to drown me instead?" The memory of my body dying while my consciousness was stuck in my memories turned my stomach.

"No. They were just too stupid to realize what was happening."

Around him, more demons appeared. Four, then six, then eight. All appearing in groups, as if they used transportation charms. Victor really had bought them all up.

My friends still weren't waking. If only the Monster had arrived before I'd tried my magic. I'd at least have blasted him away. I'd escaped him so many times before, but of course I couldn't manage that forever.

"Leave my friends," I said. "And take me."

I'd deal with getting out of his creepy dungeon when the time came. I could blow the place away with my wonky magic if my friends weren't there to get hit.

"Oh, I'm an all or nothing sort of fellow. And I want all three of you."

My skin chilled. There were now over two dozen demons. Too many for me to fight without my magic, which was too dangerous to use.

I stood shakily, reaching for Righty. So it'd be a fight, then, and I had only two daggers to use against the most powerful supernatural I'd ever met. Victor laughed as I withdrew Righty, but the sound cut off sharply a moment later.

Colored birds zipped past me out of the corner of my vision.

What the heck?

I squinted at the shapes before realization hit me. The dragonets! They dive-bombed Victor, who threw up a shield against them. One by one, they bounced off. But they shook themselves and dived again.

Thank magic they weren't flesh and blood. They couldn't be killed. Though I didn't know how effective they would be against Victor.

More figures appeared, distracting me from the dragonets. In pairs, the League of FireSouls appeared on the Everlong Portal stone.

Backup had arrived! We had a chance.

At that moment, Aidan groaned, then stood. He looked around, his sharp gaze taking in the situation. Silvery magic swirled around him, the scent of the forest rising. He transformed into a griffin, then launched himself into the air. Connor and Claire struggled to their feet as the League of FireSouls surged into the fray.

Now we really had a chance.

Something grabbed me from behind, wrapping hard around my middle.

"Let go!" I thrashed, trying to break free as it dragged me backward.

Around me, the demons were rising, shaking off their stupor.

When my feet scraped over the large circular stone that marked the portal, I shrieked, "No!"

Half a second later, I was sucked through the ether. My vision went black for a moment. When I opened my eyes, I was in the forest outside the FireSouls' compound.

I pulled away from the arm that encircled me and spun, kicking my captor in the middle before I'd even gotten a glimpse of who it was.

Corin tumbled to her back in the leaves that scattered the forest floor. I jumped onto the stone that marked the portal and envisioned the stone circle and the fight, wishing desperately to return there.

Nothing happened.

"Why the hell isn't it working?" I demanded.

"It's blocked." Corin struggled to her feet, her arm wrapped around her middle. "I think you cracked a rib."

"You deserved it. Send me back!"

"No. I can't let you be abducted."

"What about my *deirfiúr*? My friends!"

"The others will bring them here to protect them."

"What if they can't?"

"Then at least Victor won't have all of you." A hard expression entered her eyes.

"Damn it! Send me back!"

Corin shook her head. "Can't. I have orders."

Helpless rage made my skin heat and my chest feel too tight. I couldn't believe I was here, trapped, away from the fight.

The transportation charm!

I dug into my pocket and pulled out the small black stone, then threw it to the ground. But it didn't burst into the glittery cloud that would take me wherever I desired. I picked it up and chucked it again.

Nothing.

"Won't work," Corin said. "Those are blocked here."

Damn it. I shoved it back into my pocket and was about to try to call on my illusion power to scare her into following my orders when the charm around her neck made a noise.

She pressed her fingertips to the comms charm. "Yes?"

"You can bring her back. They're gone."

"On it." Corin's gaze met mine. "Your lucky day. We're going back."

"That was a fast fight." Dread filled my chest. Victor wouldn't have left without a victory, and he had more men than we'd had.

Corin joined me on the portal stone and gripped my arm. The portal sucked me in, and a moment later, I stood back in the middle of the stone circle.

Demon bodies were scattered on the ground. Only ten feet away, Connor lay on his back. I ran to him and fell to my knees, laying my fingertips at his neck.

His pulse was strong. *Thank magic.* My shoulders loosened. I glanced around, searching for everyone else. Among the bodies, I couldn't find anyone I recognized. My skin chilled.

A thud sounded behind me and I spun. Aidan's massive griffin stood in the stone circle, his coat glinting gold in the moonlight. Claire climbed off his back.

Magic shimmered around Aidan as he transformed back to human.

"They took Nix and Del," Claire said as she fell to her knees at Connor's side.

"What?" I asked.

"Almost immediately after you were dragged away, Victor changed tactics," Aidan said. "I was nearest Claire, so I picked her up. Before I could reach Nix or Del, Victor's demons grabbed them. They disappeared a moment later."

"Damn it!" Fear clawed at my chest. "He must have taken them to the waypoint." My dragon sense couldn't find them there.

Connor shifted and opened his eyes, croaking, "What happened?"

"You got knocked out, dummy," Claire said.

Alton approached. "But it kept you alive. The demons assumed you were dead and left you alone."

I whirled on Alton. "You bastards! You dragged me off when I could have helped."

Alton's gaze chilled me. "We did what was necessary. And there were too many for you to be any help."

"Your magic is, uh, pretty powerful, Cass," Connor said. "Probably better you didn't use it a second time. My insides feel liquefied."

"Yeah," Claire added. "At least this way, Nix and Del are still alive."

I stutter-stepped backward. They were right. I could have killed them. In my fear and my rage, I could have let loose again with magic I didn't understand.

"I'm sorry," I croaked. "I—I—"

"It's cool." Claire rubbed my arm. "You were just trying to help."

I scrubbed a hand over my face, thinking about Del and Nix. "We've got to get them back." Victor Orriodor made his home at a strange place that wasn't on Earth. It was between the heavens and hells and impossible for me to find.

"Do you know how to get to the waypoint where Victor Orriodor lives?" I asked Alton.

"No. We do not," Alton said.

I wanted to scream my frustration. But I didn't have time to lose my shit. My *deirfiúr* needed me. I had to find them.

Find them.

Of course. My FireSoul abilities hadn't been able to locate the waypoint in the past, but maybe now that they had the extra power, they could.

"Will you guys step back?" I asked. "Far away. I'm going to try to use my new strength to find Nix and Del."

Everyone nodded and walked away, well outside of the stone circle. I was really going to have to get a handle on my new magic, because I didn't want to be a walking bomb.

But at least I had it back.

It wasn't hard to shove away all thoughts and focus on my dragon sense. I'd never wanted to find anything so badly in all my life.

Within a few seconds, I picked up the thread of their location.

But it wasn't at the waypoint.

"They're in Magic's Bend," I said, confusion welling.

"What the hell?" Aidan stepped forward.

The others followed, gathering around me in a large group—Aidan, Claire, Connor, and the nine FireSouls I'd met before. The dragonets hovered over everyone's heads.

"Yeah, I'm sure of it." No wonder it'd been easy to pick up the thread of their location. They weren't at the waypoint. "Let's go."

"We cannot follow," Alton said. "The Order of the Magica has a strong presence in Magic's Bend. The League is already too small. If we are captured, we will disappear for good."

"And then there'd be no one to rescue *us* from the Prison for Magical Miscreants," Corin said.

I remembered what they'd said about that being one of their primary goals. Of course they couldn't risk their entire organization.

"But when Victor removes them from Magic's Bend, contact us," Alton said. "We can help you at the waypoint, or another place that is removed from the Order's influence."

"Here." Corin handed me a transportation charm. "Use this. It's the least we can do."

"Thank you." They were committed to keeping me and my *deirfiúr* out of Victor's hands, but not to the point that they'd risk their organization. I couldn't blame them. "I will let you know what happens and if we need help."

They nodded and departed, disappearing in pairs through the portal. Within moments, we stood alone in the stone circle, the moon shining serenely as if the ground weren't singed and soaked with blood.

The bodies of the fallen demons had all disappeared, so it was too late to check them for transportation charms. At least we had two and the one from Corin. Enough to get us back and then some.

Aidan bent and picked up the dampening cuff I'd discarded. He handed it to me. "This might come in handy now. Maybe dampen some of your power so you can control it."

I smiled and put it on. Calm descended over me as it diminished some of the crazy-strong power ricocheting around inside me. Hopefully with this thing, I could perform something closer to normal magic. The kind that didn't come with a sonic boom.

"I think it works," I said. Until I learned to control the strength of my new power, it'd be better if I was at a slightly lower intensity.

"Back to Magic's Bend?" I asked. "We've got a rescue mission to pull off."

CHAPTER THIRTEEN

We arrived back in Magic's Bend a few moments later. Because of the time change, it was early evening, the hour when the light turns to dark. I hadn't been able to tell precisely where my *deirfiúr* were from so far away, so we'd transported to my living room.

Connor held up his empty bag. "I'm running to my workshop. I need to refill my potion bombs."

"Get something that'll work as a mask," I said. "If that building isn't empty, we don't want to be recognized."

He nodded. "Good idea."

"Grab one for me," Claire said.

"And meet us at my car." I shrugged out of the coat Aidan had loaned me and said, "Let me grab a jacket and masks. Help yourself to anything. I'll be out in a sec and we'll go."

Not that there'd be much in my fridge or pantry, but they were probably starving. It'd been ages since we'd eaten.

I hurried into my room and grabbed the first jacket I saw. It was draped over the bed, a discard from earlier. As I tugged it on, my golden dampener cuff glinted on my wrist.

I scavenged in my dresser for a couple old ski hats. I found two black ones—very robber-chic—and pulled them out. There was a pair of scissors lying on my dresser, and I used them to cut eye holes.

I returned to the living room to find Claire and Aidan eating granola bars and chugging soda. Claire tossed me one, and I tore into it, shoving a bite into my mouth before mumbling, "Ready?"

"Let's get them," Claire said.

I grabbed my keys on the way out, and we hurried down the stairs, polishing off our impromptu dinner. I ate because it was probably a good idea, not because I was hungry. But I was so rocky with worry that it was hard to swallow.

When we stepped out into the dark night, a drizzly rain chilled the air. Connor jogged up the sidewalk to join us, carefully cradling the messenger bag that now bulged with his ammo.

I closed my eyes and called on my dragon sense. It pinged with recognition, that familiar tug pulling me down the street and toward the center of town.

"The business district?" I said. That was the last place I'd expected.

"What the hell are they doing there?" Connor asked.

"It'd be quiet this time of night," Aidan said. "And it's a weekend, I believe. Not a bad place for a secret meeting."

"Let's go." I crossed the street toward Cecelia.

We hopped in, Aidan next to me and Connor and Claire in the back. I said a little prayer as the engine coughed and sputtered, but it turned over.

Thank magic.

I drove like a maniac through town, keeping my eyes out for cops and pedestrians. Fate favored us tonight, and no cops pulled us over.

When we neared the business district, I nodded to a tall gray building in front of us. "It's that one."

"Take the next turn," Aidan said. "There's an overflow lot where people park for O'Connel's, a local bar. We can park there so he won't see us coming."

I nodded, my gaze caught by the many windows that were blacked out like dead eyes. The building was mostly empty, but I didn't want Victor to be looking out a window and see us come in.

And if we were going to be breaking and entering, it'd be better if Cecelia wasn't sitting right outside like a beacon.

I pulled into the lot, which was appropriately dark, and turned the car off. I pocketed the keys and sucked in a deep breath.

Aidan squeezed my leg and said, "We'll get them, Cass."

I gave him a small smile, the most I was capable of right now, but I appreciated the gesture.

"Yeah," I said. "We will."

"So weird they're in there, though," Connor said. "Evil masterminds hiding out somewhere boring like the business district?"

"Not that weird, actually," Claire joked. "Ask anyone where the bad guys are hiding during a recession."

I laughed, but it was an awkward, nervous sound. I'd take a snake-filled, demon-infested temple any day over this kind of terror.

Before getting out of the car, I turned around to look at my companions. "Okay, I'll lead. We move quickly and quietly."

"And shoot to kill," Aidan said.

"Happy to," Claire answered.

"Delighted," Connor added.

I handed a ski mask to Aidan and pulled mine over my head, adjusting it so I could see out the eye holes. It was itchy and awkward.

"I feel like a low-rent robber," I said.

"You look like one, too," Claire said.

I grinned at her. She'd pulled hers on as well. None of us looked good, but it didn't matter. I didn't want to be recognized by the security cameras. That'd be a one-way trip to the Prison for Magical Miscreants. I'd only used my powers in Magic's Bend a couple times in the past because I was so afraid of revealing myself to the Order of the Magica. Having security footage of my face breaking into this building—where I'd also be breaking out the magic—would be really bad. Aidan could only shift into animals, which was too bad. If he could shapeshift into another human, I could mirror that and avoid this damned mask.

Silently, we climbed out of the car and slipped through the shadows to the alley. It was quiet and dark back here. No one bothered to come to this part of town at this hour. Like Connor had said, it was boring.

The alley fed out to a small street that lined the back of our target building. It was one way, and there were no cars, thankfully.

Connor pointed to the heavy metal back entrance and the camera above it. "Let me freeze that security camera first."

"Good idea."

Connor raced across the street and melted into the shadows at the edge of the building, careful to stay out of range of the camera. When he was about a dozen feet away, he reached into his bag and pulled out a round bottle. With expert skill, he chucked the bomb at the camera.

It shattered over the camera, and a sparkly silver fluid spread over it. Connor gestured for us to cross.

"It'll look like static to the security guard," Connor said when we joined him.

"Thanks," I said.

We approached the heavy metal door. It was some kind of service entrance, which was perfect for our needs. There shouldn't be a security guard on the other side—just at the front to check people in and out.

"Do we need the penatrist charms?" I whispered.

"I can handle it." Aidan pulled his spell stripper out of his pocket and ran the small silver charm around the edges of the door. Once again, I was grateful that he was only mostly a good guy.

Good where it counted, at least, which was always on my side.

The prickly feeling of the protective spell that guarded the door faded, and Aidan put the spell stripper back into his pocket.

I grabbed his hand before he could turn the handle and said, "If we're outnumbered, you guys need to run for it."

"No way," Claire said.

"I mean it. If any of us get caught, someone has to stay free to rescue them. I'm not saying ditch entirely, but pick your battles."

"Don't be so negative," Connor said. "We can do this."

"Yeah." But I didn't have a good feeling about any of it.

I nodded at Aidan, who turned the handle and entered on silent feet, then held it open for the rest of us.

We slipped into the building like thieves. I wasn't used to breaking and entering into anything modern.

"I prefer tombs. This modern B&E makes me nervous." I hoped that was all it was, not some sense of foreboding.

I led us down the dimly-lit hall. Our footsteps were silent on the industrial grade carpet. It didn't take long to find a set of stairs, and we began the climb.

"They're near the top," I whispered back to my friends.

My dragon sense tugged hard at the fifteenth floor. I was gasping by the time I pushed open the door, not used to the climbing. As soon as we'd all made it out of the stairwell, a security guard turned into our hall. His eyes widened when he saw us, and my heart jumped into my throat.

"Duck!" Connor whispered.

I crouched low, and Connor threw a potion bomb over my head. It exploded on the man's chest. Surprise flashed in his eyes before they rolled back in his head, and he tumbled like an oak tree onto his back.

"Sleeping potion," Connor whispered. "He'll be out for a few hours."

"Good choice." I'd seen Connor's potion bombs do some nasty things, and I was grateful he'd gone with something more benign. No reason to kill a guy just doing his job, as long as he didn't work for Victor Orriodor.

Sure, I wanted to commit murder. But only Victor. Everyone else was in the way, but I didn't want them to get hurt unless it was the only way to save Del or Nix. The fact that I'd throw anyone under the bus for my *deirfiúr* was bloodthirsty, but it was the truth.

I gestured to my friends, and we continued down the hall, our footsteps light. My heart pounded in my ears as we neared Nix and Del. They had to be alive because my dragon sense picked them up, but that didn't guarantee they were unharmed.

The scent of rot rolled toward us down the hall, and the now-familiar feel of bee stings on my skin made my muscles tense.

Victor. His awful magic was so distinct that there was no mistaking him. I picked up on another scent, too, a sickly sweet aroma. Disgusting. I gagged. There was also the feeling of sweaty palms, which was one of the worst magical signatures I'd ever felt.

I shook off the gross feeling and crept forward. But I bounced off an invisible wall, my nose hurting like hell.

"Barrier," I whispered. It was strong magic, too. I turned to Aidan and held out a hand. He passed me a penatrist charm and kept one for himself.

We slipped through, then handed them back to Connor and Claire. They came through, then each handed a penatrist charm to Aidan and me. I shoved mine into my pocked and crept down the hall on silent feet, my friends at my back.

We had to be close if there was a special barrier here.

The sound of low voices drifted down the hall. I halted right before a massive glass wall that probably led into an office, and everyone else stopped behind.

We were near the corner of the building, so perhaps there was a big office here. I peeked through the glass, trying to keep as much of me hidden behind the wall as possible.

Within, Nix and Del slumped on a couch, passed out and wearing collars of some sort. Slave collars that would bind them to Victor, perhaps, or magic-dampening collars.

The bastard himself lounged in a chair in front of a massive desk. The figure behind the desk looked vaguely familiar. A large man with heavy jowls, he looked about sixty. His piercing blue eyes were cold and dead. The sickly sweet smell came from him. The sweaty hands feeling, too.

Magica.

It hit me then. This bulldog of a man had been walking on the stage at the Nullifier's memorial. He was from the Order.

So, Victor really was working with the Order. Or at least, one of them.

I strained to hear what they were saying through the glass.

"I can get the other," Victor said. "We can still make this work."

I had to be the *other*. But make what work?

"I put my faith in you, Victor," the bulldog grumbled. "And it's taking longer than promised. How can I trust that you'll finish the job? My support is costly, as I'm sure you know."

"I brought them here to prove to you that things are moving along." Victor's voice sounded cold.

The bulldog's brows lowered over his eyes. No doubt he was used to people bowing and scraping before him, considering his position in the Order. But Victor wasn't the type to do that, even if he did need the bulldog. He was too proud.

I shoved aside my desire to loiter and eavesdrop. Nix and Del were unconscious. If they needed medical attention that I'd delayed because I was curious, I'd never forgive myself.

But I'd have to try to win this with my daggers instead of magic. Even if the bulldog couldn't see my face, I didn't want to alert an Order member that magic as strong as mine existed.

"What the hell—"

The gravelly voice sounded from behind. I spun to look. A massive man loomed over us. I reached for my dagger, but his huge hand swept out and knocked me across the cheek. I went flying, pain blaring in my face.

In a flash, Aidan threw a fireball that consumed the man, but it was too late. We'd lost any element of surprise. Footsteps thundered down the hall, probably men working for the bulldog or Victor.

I scrambled to my feet. On the other side of the glass, the bulldog and Victor surged to their feet. Two guards, whom I hadn't seen because of their positioning, whirled on us. Connor threw a potion bomb at one, and Claire threw a blast of fire at another. They dropped to the ground.

If we could get Del and Nix before the backup got here, we could maybe make a run for it.

I gestured to Connor and Claire, pointing them to Del and Nix. "Get them. We'll distract the others."

I was careful not to say their names for fear of leading the Order of the Magica back to them. A swirl of gray light surrounded Aidan, and he shifted into a massive black leopard, not his signature griffin. Probably to hide his identity, I realized.

Aidan launched himself through the glass window into the office. It shattered and crashed to the ground as he charged Victor, who threw his signature sonic boom.

Aidan dodged it by an inch, but I felt the reverberations when it slammed into the hallway wall behind him.

Connor and Claire rushed into the room, headed straight for Del and Nix, who hadn't woken.

Acting on instinct, I hurled a dagger at the bulldog, but he threw up a hand and blocked it. The blade clattered to the ground. The footsteps of approaching guards grew nearer.

"You think you can rescue your friends, FireSoul?" Victor asked coldly.

I didn't bother answering, but called my dagger back to me and flung Lefty at the bulldog again. It pierced him in the shoulder and he howled.

Connor and Claire had grabbed Del and Nix, draping them over their shoulders in a fireman's carry. As they dragged them toward the door, Aidan lunged at Victor again, this time getting his arm and shoulder in his massive jaws.

Victor roared, his face twisted with pain. Aidan shook him, clamping down harder, but Victor's magic swelled on the air, the scent of rot overwhelming. A moment later, he disappeared from between Aidan's jaws, no doubt realizing that staying meant being torn apart.

With Victor gone, we almost had this!

But the sound of the guards' footsteps were too close, and there had to be at least a dozen of them. The bulldog had pulled the blade from his shoulder, and his eyes were wild with rage. His sickly sweet magic surged, as if he were loading up a big spell with whatever his gift was. We'd already discovered that he could create force fields, but I thought he was planning something more violent. I glanced out the gaping hole where the massive glass window had been.

A dozen guards were charging up the hall, their magic signatures rolling toward us. They were strong, and there were a lot of them. More magical signatures came from another direction, perhaps from the floor below. We had to escape both groups.

"Get them out of here!" I shouted. "I'll hold off the guards."

I reached for the bulldog's gift over force fields. He'd protected himself from my first blade, so I just had to create a massive one to hold the guards off.

Aidan's massive head swung toward me, disbelief in his golden eyes.

"Go!" I begged. I put everything I had into the word, every promise that this meant more to me than anything else and that I'd never forgive him if he didn't get my *deirfiúr* out of here. "I can feel more guards on the other floor. You have to protect them so they can escape. I'll follow!"

Aidan cocked his head as if searching for the magical signatures of the other guards I'd felt. They had strong magic—it rolled over my skin in waves—and I could tell when he felt them.

He nodded, his gaze intense and angry, then charged the door. I caught a glimpse of Connor and Claire fleeing with Del and Nix. Aidan had their back. They'd probably run into the other group of guards, but I had to have faith in Aidan.

If I failed at this and let them catch me, the bulldog knew what I was. I'd end up in the Prison for Magical Miscreants. Or a prisoner of Victor Orriodor. I didn't know what was worse, but I didn't care.

I raced into the hall, blocking the way my friends had fled, and turned back to the guards who ran toward me. They were only twenty feet away. The bulldog charged toward the office door, coming for me with whatever magic he possessed.

I wanted to throw off the dampening charm and blast them, but my friends were still too close.

I pulled on the bulldog's magic, envisioning a barrier between myself and the guards. I just had to block them from my friends. I thrust my hands forward and gave the force field everything I had, trying to keep control just in case the dampening charm didn't work.

Magic flowed, silvery and bright, creating a sparkling, transparent wall between me and my enemies. My chest ached with the amount of power I was trying to control, and my breath grew short. The bulldog threw out his hands, hurling whatever magic he'd been building up.

A hurricane hit my force field, massive wind and rain that nearly blasted a hole in my shield. The collision vibrated up my arms and I nearly lost control of the force field. It held up, but barely.

"You FireSoul bitch!" the bulldog yelled. He was a weather witch, and I cringed to think of what he'd create next.

The guards attacked, throwing fire and ice and even a swarm of bees. Each hit the force field and made my arms shake, stealing a bit more of my strength. I couldn't throw off the dampening charm while trying to hold up the barrier, so I'd just have to hope they'd run out of strength before I did. Then I could lower it, throw off the dampener charm, and blast them with my crazy power.

But from the way I was shaking, I didn't know if I'd make it. My vision blacked out for a moment. I stumbled to my knees as more magic hit the force field, but I kept it raised, focusing my eyes on the glittery light of the barrier. I could barely see it through the blindness stealing over my vision as my muscles turned to jelly.

As my family had said, I had unlimited power, but not the physical strength or practice to wield it.

A tornado jumped from the hands of the bulldog, a howling cyclone of wind that pulled office furniture into its clutches. My magic faltered.

I'm a dead woman.

I chanced a quick glance over my shoulder, wondering if my friends had gotten far enough away. I caught sight of a guard's face just before he plowed into me, driving me into the carpet.

I hadn't shielded my back. My face was pressed into the carpet with the guard pressing a heavy knee into my back. I peered up at the hallway. My force field died, the glittering light fading away entirely, and the rest of the guards surged toward us.

Prison-strength magic dampening cuffs slammed around my wrists, sapping my power, just as something heavy hit me in the head.

I blacked out.

CHAPTER FOURTEEN

Oh shit, oh shit, oh shit.

The refrain filled my mind as soon as consciousness woke me from a slumber as deep as death. Flashes of vague memories filled my mind. The bulldog's guards bundling me up and tossing me in the back of a car. Endless travel. An angry male voice speaking to someone on a comms charm or phone. He'd lost someone. Two someones.

The bulldog hadn't gotten Nix or Del! Nor had Victor. My *deirfiúr* had escaped. A victorious grin stretched over my face as more memories flowed into my mind. Flashes of a stone wall passing by my face as I was dragged down a corridor. Being thrown into a cell and the stone scraping against my skin.

The memories ended there, and I knew I was in trouble even before I opened my eyes.

When I did force them open, I wasn't surprised to see a dimly lit stone ceiling above me. The walls and floor were also stone and the air icy cold. It could have been Victor Orriodor's dungeon, except for the small window high in the wall. Behind metal bars, the moon gleamed, full and bright.

No, this wasn't Victor's dungeon. That was underground, and there was no moon to see even if there had been a window. The waypoint lacked a moon or sun.

I was in the Prison for Magical Miscreants. And I didn't feel an ounce of the fear I'd expected to feel if I ever ended up here.

No doubt, my situation was bad. I was wearing nothing but a black jumpsuit. No boots, no dagger, not even my dampening charm. Nor the prison-strength magical dampening cuffs they'd slapped on me before knocking me out.

I climbed off the hard, skinny bed I'd been lying on and grinned as I looked around. I probably looked insane, but I didn't care.

If they'd taken my dampening charm and removed the cuffs, they didn't know what I was. Sure, they might know I was a FireSoul. But they had no idea what I was capable of if they'd been stupid enough to take the charm and cuffs away.

I touched the wall, feeling for whatever protective spells shrouded my cell. There was a magic dampening spell, of course. No way they'd remove the cuffs if there wasn't. There'd been one at Victor's dungeon and at the magical fight club holding cells I'd once rescued Nix and Del from. The spell was standard issue and repressed any magic that the prisoners might possess.

Idiots. That might have held me once, but no longer.

I stretched my hands, wiggling my fingers. Power sparked in my veins so much that the cell couldn't contain it.

A rustling sound came from the corner of the cell. I peered into the dark, my eye catching movement.

A fat little rat scurried forward, his dark eyes gleaming. He was white and black, with a friendly look to him. I crouched down and held out a hand, grinning.

"Hey, little guy," I whispered. I liked rodents.

The rat hopped onto my hand and stood on his back legs, pink nose twitching as he met my gaze.

A flash of an image filled my mind—a man, sitting in a cell like mine, his black jumpsuit ragged—and a voice echoed in my ear.

"Who are you?" the voice asked.

The voice had to be from the man in my vision. I tried to focus on his face. I recognized him. The FireSoul I'd seen at the Alpha Council stronghold last month. At that time, they'd been dragging him off to this prison for the crime of being a FireSoul. So this wasn't a vision, exactly. Was this rat was showing me someone else in another cell here?

"What's going on?" I asked. "How are we speaking?"

"I'm an Anima Mage. The rats do my bidding, exploring for me, speaking on my behalf. You're holding Rufus. Ralph, his brother, is here with me. We're communicating through them."

I looked at the fat little rat in my hand, then at the skinny guy within my mind's eye. "You must feed them well."

"They're my friends."

I liked this dude already. Anyone who counted rodents among his buddies was a good guy. I'd heard of Anima Mages before. They could force animals to do their bidding, but he made friends with them instead.

"How are you?" he asked again.

"I'm Cass Clereaux. I mean, McFane," I whispered. "You're the FireSoul who was captured at the Alpha Council."

He nodded as if he knew I could see him. "What are you?"

"I'm a FireSoul, too."

"That's not what they said."

"Who?"

"The guards who brought you here. They said you were a thief, but they didn't know your name or magical species."

"Interesting."

"But it's odd they didn't say you were a FireSoul."

"It is?"

"Yes. Normally we're their favorite to torment."

So, the prison didn't know what I was? Did that mean the bulldog had kept it a secret? It seemed they didn't know my name, but they did know what I was capable of. Yet they hadn't reported that to the prison. Was he running a side job with Victor, while keeping the rest of the Order in the dark about what I was? Things were looking better and better.

"How do you know all this?" I asked.

"I explore the prison through Ralph and Rufus. They see a lot."

"What's your name?"

"Emile," he said.

"Nice to meet you, Emile. And Ralph and Rufus. We're going to be breaking out of here soon."

His gaze brightened. "Yeah? Were you sent by the League of FireSouls to rescue me?"

"No, but we'll manage all the same." I looked up at the window, at the moon outside. "And I'll have people coming for me."

My friends would find me, if I didn't escape first. I knew I could count on that.

"That works for me," Emile said.

"I'll talk to you soon, Emile." I set down Rufus, and he scurried away, back through the little hole in the wall.

I stood and looked around my cell. My worst fears had come true. My parents were dead. At least one member of the Order of the Magica knew I was a FireSoul. I was in the Prison for Magical Miscreants.

But my face wasn't leaking. There were no tears despite the fact that all the worst shit had hit the fan.

Actually, I felt pretty damned good. I was facing my fears, and they weren't so bad. My *deirfiúr* were alive and free, and I had a tidal wave of magic flowing through my veins.

I didn't know what Victor or the Order had planned for me, but I was going to find out. And if they thought they could keep me locked up in this place, they were too damned wrong.

I was coming for them. And they'd better be scared.

THANK YOU FOR READING!

Want to find out how Cass and her *deirfiúr* got the money to start their shop? Sign up for my newsletter to get an exclusive copy of *Hidden Magic,* which is only available to subscribers. You can go to www.LinseyHall.com/subscribe to sign up.

The next book will be out in September, so keep an eye out!

If you'd like to know more about the inspiration for the Dragon's Gift series, please read on for the Author's Note.

AUTHOR'S NOTE

I hope you enjoyed reading *Eternal Magic*. I love writing these books, because they combine my two lives—that as a writer and as an archaeologist.

As with my other stories, *Eternal Magic* features historical sites. In fact, this one probably features more than any other. In some places, I try to stick very close to history. In others, I make things up. So if you're interested in knowing what was real and what wasn't, read on.

First, the pyramid. This was based on my own personal research into Egyptian Pyramids and also on the knowledge provided by my friend, archaeologist Veronica Morris, who has worked on Egyptian archaeological sites. Considering that all my research was done via computer and she's actually worked on the sites, she provided all the really good stuff :-)

The treasure room was based on King Tut's tomb, which was discovered in 1922 and was filled with furniture, ornate boxes, and many artifacts. The Bastet statue she found was made of alabaster, the most common material for carved depictions of Bastet.

Of the boobytraps that Cass and Del faced, the hematite powder and razor wire may have been actual Egyptian booby traps. When the Bahariya Oasis tomb was explored by archaeologists in 2001, they found an eight-inch thick layer of hematite powder at the sarcophagus. I was only able to find one (not very good) reference to razor wire being used in pyramids, so it could be totally fake. It was neat, though, so I thought I'd include it. And I'd rather write the next Cass adventure than do in-depth research to prove that razor wire actually was used, so I leave it up to you to decide if you want to believe it was real or not.

But by far the most interesting part of Cass's journey through the pyramid was her adventure with the boat. I'm a nautical archaeologist, so this part is my favorite. Several boats have been found buried at pyramid complexes. The boat that I used as particular inspiration for this scene was the Khufu ship, which was buried in a pit in the Giza pyramid complex around 2500 BC. The exact purpose of the boat is unknown, though it may have been meant to carry the resurrected Khufu to the afterlife. The dead may have also possessed magical items to defend themselves against dangers on the way.

Everything that I wrote about Cass's boat was taken from history (except the magical river:-)). There actually were symbols carved into the wood of pyramid boats to help with the reconstruction, just like a shelf from Ikea comes with stickers to indicate which side of the board goes where. The timbers were lashed together with ropes, and the planks even had roughly jagged edges that helped avoid slippage. This jogged-plank feature was found on the Abydos boats, discovered in 2000, rather than on Khufu's barge, but it was such a neat feature that I had to include it. The little chips of wood that Cass and Del left on the floor because they couldn't figure out where they belonged were actually tenons, little pieces of wood that fit into slots called mortises in order to keep the planks nicely lined up and firmly in place. For Cass's purposes, the boat still would have worked, though you wouldn't want to go to sea in a boat that didn't have them if it was supposed to.

The riddle that Cass and Del had to answer to get past the Sphinx was an old (and I mean *old*) Sumerian riddle, one of twenty-five found inscribed on a clay tablet discovered at Sumer, the southernmost region of the ancient Mesopotamia, which is now modern day Iraq and Kuwait. The tablet was dated to the 18th century BC (see? Super old). I'd have chosen an Egyptian riddle, but I couldn't find one.

The enchanted Celtic cauldron that Victor Orriodor stole was based on the Gundestrop Cauldron, a silver, Iron Age artifact that was found in a bog in Denmark. Specifically, it was part of the La Tene culture and was most likely laid in the bog as a sacrificial item between 150-1BC. I've always loved Celtic history and I was lucky enough to see the cauldron on a research trip to Denmark and Ireland, so I wanted to include it in the book. Any place that I can slip in real history or artifacts, I like to do so. Check out my Pinterest Page (under

Linsey Hall) for pictures of this ornate, beautifully decorated cauldron.

The Lyceum of Metis is an entirely made up place, of course, but the origin of the name is interesting. A lyceum is an educational institution and the name is actually a Latin version of the Ancient Greek word Lykeion. Metis was one of the ancient Greek titans. In the fifth century BC, during the height of Greek philosophy, Metis was considered the mother of wisdom.

The passage tomb that Cass visited to find out about her past is based on two passage tombs that I visited in Ireland as part of research. Newgrange, the largest one, and Cairn T at Loughcrew, were both well preserved examples of these tombs and it was possible to enter them, which was really quite amazing considering that they are as old as the pyramids. As I wrote in *Eternal Magic,* the tombs often had a big stone blocking the entrance that one had to climb over (both of the tombs I entered were easier to access). The exterior stone was decorated with swirling stone carving and the interior stones in the main chambers were often carved with swirls and flowers. There were stone basins within the small interior rooms, which contained bones and artifacts when the tombs were originally excavated. But the most amazing part was the light that shined through the light shaft at solstice. I wished I had seen the real thing, but the reproduction that I experienced was amazing in itself and I just had to include it in a book.

That's it for the historical and archaeological sites featured in *Eternal Magic.* But one of the most important things about the *Dragon's Gift* series is Cass's relationship with the artifacts and the sense of responsibility she feels to protect them. I spoke about this in the Author's Note for the other books in the series, so this part might be repetitive for some folks (feel free to quit now if so), but I want to include it in each of my Author's Notes because it's so important to me.

I knew I had a careful line to tread when writing these books—combining the ethics of archaeology with the fantasy aspect of treasure hunting isn't always easy.

There is a big difference between these two activities. As much as I value artifacts, they are not treasure. Not even the gold artifacts. They are pieces of our history that contain valuable information, and as such, they belong to all of us. Every artifact that is excavated should be properly conserved and stored in a museum so that everyone can have access to our history. No single person can own history, and I believe very strongly that individuals should not own artifacts. Treasure hunting is the pursuit of artifacts for personal gain.

So why did I make Cass Cleraux a treasure hunter? I'd have loved to call her an archaeologist, but nothing about Cass's work is like archaeology. Archaeology is a very laborious, painstaking process—and it certainly doesn't involve selling artifacts. That wouldn't work for the fast-paced, adventurous series that I had planned for *Dragon's Gift*. Not to mention the fact that dragons are famous for coveting treasure. Considering where Cass got her skills, it just made sense to call her a treasure hunter (though I really like to think of her as a magic hunter). Even though I write urban fantasy, I strive for accuracy. Cass doesn't engage in archaeological practices—therefore, I cannot call her an archaeologist. I also have a duty as an archaeologist to properly represent my field and our goals—namely, to protect and share history. Treasure hunting doesn't do this. One of the biggest battles that archaeology faces today is protecting cultural heritage from thieves.

I debated long and hard about not only what to call Cass, but also about how she would do her job. I wanted it to involve all the cool things we think about when we think about archaeology—namely, the Indiana Jones stuff, whether it's real or not. Because that stuff is fun, and my main goal is to write a fun book. But I didn't know quite how to do that while still staying within the bounds of my own ethics. I can cut myself and other writers some slack because this is fiction, but I couldn't go too far into smash-and-grab treasure hunting.

I consulted some of my archaeology colleagues to get their take, which was immensely helpful. Wayne Lusardi, the State Maritime Archaeologist for Michigan, and Douglas Inglis and Veronica Morris, both archaeologists for Interactive Heritage, were immensely helpful with ideas. My biggest problem was figuring out how to have Cass steal artifacts from tombs and then sell them and still sleep at night. Everything I've just said is pretty counter to this, right?

That's where the magic comes in. Cass isn't after the artifacts themselves (she puts them back where she found them, if you recall)—she's after the magic that the artifacts contain. She's more of a magic hunter than a treasure hunter. That solved a big part of my problem. At least she was putting the artifacts back. Though that's not proper archaeology (especially the damage she sometimes causes, which she always goes back to fix), I could let it pass. At least it's clear that she believes she shouldn't keep the artifact or harm the site. But the SuperNerd in me said, "Well, that magic is part of the artifact's context. It's important to the artifact and shouldn't be removed and sold."

Now *that* was a problem. I couldn't escape my SuperNerd self, so I was in a real conundrum. Fortunately, that's where the immensely intelligent Wayne Lusardi came in. He suggested that the magic could have an expiration date. If the magic wasn't used before it decayed, it could cause huge problems. Think explosions and tornado spells run amok. It could ruin the entire site, not to mention possibly cause injury and death. That would be very bad.

So now you see why Cass Clereaux didn't just steal artifacts to sell them. Not only is selling the magic cooler, it's also better from an ethical standpoint, especially if the magic was going to cause problems in the long run. These aren't perfect solutions—the perfect solution would be sending in a team of archaeologists to carefully record the site and remove the dangerous magic—but that wouldn't be a very fun book. Hopefully this was a good compromise that you enjoyed (and that my old professors don't hang their heads over).

Thank you so much for reading *Eternal Magic*, and if you've made it this far in the Author's Note, thank you for reading this as well! It's an important part of the story and I appreciate when folks take the time to learn about the archaeological influences in my books. I hope you'll stay with Cass on her journey, because it's not done yet!

DEDICATION

For Jon Thomas, the coolest kid I know.

ACKNOWLEDGMENTS

Thank you, Ben, for everything you've done to support me. Thank you to Carol Thomas for sharing your thoughts on the book and being amazing inspiration. My books are always better because of your help.

I'd like to thank my good friend and archaeologist Veronica Morris for her help with the pyramid scene in the beginning. Though I made up a lot of the fun booby traps, she helped me with ideas and figuring out what was accurate. It was my friend and fellow archaeologist Doug Inglis's idea to have the hieroglyphs come to life.

The Dragon's Gift series is a product of my two lives: one as an archaeologist and one as a novelist. I'd like to thank my friends, Wayne Lusardi, the State Maritime Archaeologist for Michigan, and Douglas Inglis and Veronica Morris, both archaeologists for Interactive Heritage, for their ideas about how to have a treasure hunter heroine that doesn't conflict too much with archaeology's ethics. The Author's Note contains a bit more about this if you are interested.

Thank you to Jena O'Connor and Lindsey Loucks for various forms of editing. The book is immensely better because of you!

And finally, Cass says the phrase "many hands made light work." My great grandmother, Frances Sontheim, used to say this, and now my family does as well, so I wanted to include it. Also, when Cass pulls open a heavy wooden door, it's a reference to the Coconut Grove, a story that my grandfather, Bob Hall, used to tell about why all doors in America open outward. It's a sad story so I won't share it here, but the reference was to him. I wouldn't be who I am without my family, and there would certainly be no Dragon's Gift books.

GLOSSARY

Alpha Council - There are two governments that enforce law for supernaturals—the Alpha Council and the Order of the Magica. The Alpha Council governs all shifters. They work cooperatively with Alpha Council when necessary - for example, when capturing FireSouls.

Blood Sorceress - A type of Magica who can create magic using blood.

Conjurer - A Magica who uses magic to create something from nothing. They cannot create magic, but if there is magic around them, they can put that magic into their conjuration.

Dark Magic - The kind that is meant to harm. It's not necessarily bad, but it often is.

Deirfiúr - Sisters in Irish.

Demons - Often employed to do evil. They live in various hells but can be released upon the earth if you know how to get to them and then get them out. If they are killed on earth, they are sent back to their hell.

Dragon Sense - A FireSoul's ability to find treasure. It is an internal sense pulls them toward what they seek. It is easiest to find gold, but they can find anything or anyone that is valued by someone.

Elemental Mage – A rare type of mage who can manipulate all of the elements.

Enchanted Artifacts – Artifacts can be imbued with magic that lasts after the death of the person who put the magic into the artifact (unlike a spell that has not been put into an artifact—these spells disappear after the Magica's death). But magic is not stable. After a period of time—hundreds or thousands of years depending on the circumstance—the magic will degrade. Eventually, it can go bad and cause many problems.

Fire Mage – A mage who can control fire.

FireSoul - A very rare type of Magica who shares a piece of the dragon's soul. They can locate treasure and steal the gifts (powers) of other supernaturals. With practice, they can manipulate the gifts they steal, becoming the strongest of that gift. They are despised and feared. If they are caught, they are thrown in the Prison of Magical Deviants.

The Great Peace - The most powerful piece of magic ever created. It hides magic from the eyes of humans.

Heart of Glencarrough - The child who tends the Heartstone.

Hearth Witch – A Magica who is versed in magic relating to hearth and home. They are often good and potions and protective spells and are also very perceptive when on their own turf.

Heartstone - A charm that protects Glencarrough, the Alpha Council stronghold, from dark magic. It was created through the sacrifice of many shifters and must be tended by the Heart of Glencarrough, a child.

Magica - Any supernatural who has the power to create magic—witches, sorcerers, mages. All are governed by the Order of the Magica.

Mirror Mage - A Magica who can temporarily borrow the powers of other supernaturals. They can mimic the powers as long as they are near the other supernatural. Or they can hold onto the power, but once they are away from the other supernatural, they can only use it once.

The Origin - The descendent of the original alpha shifter. They are the most powerful shifter and can turn into any species.

Order of the Magica - There are two governments that enforce law for supernaturals—the Alpha Council and the Order of the Magica. The Order of the Magica govern all Magica. They work cooperatively with Alpha Council when necessary - for example, when capturing FireSouls.

Phantom - A type of supernatural that is similar to a ghost. They are incorporeal. They feed off the misery and pain of others, forcing them to relive their greatest nightmares and fears. They do not have a fully functioning mind like a human or supernatural. Rather, they are a shadow of their former selves. Half bloods are extraordinarily rare.

Scroll of Truths - A compendium of knowledge about the strongest supernaturals. It is a prophetic scroll that includes information about future powerful beings.

Seeker - A type of supernatural who can find things. FireSouls often pass off their dragon sense as Seeker power.

Shifter - A supernatural who can turn into an animal. All are governed by the Alpha Council.

Transporter - A type of supernatural who can travel anywhere. Their power is limited and must regenerate after each use.

ABOUT LINSEY

Before becoming a writer, Linsey was an archaeologist who studied shipwrecks in all kinds of water, from the tropics to muddy rivers (and she has a distinct preference for one over the other). After a decade of tromping around in search of old bits of stuff, she settled down to started penning her own adventure novels and is freaking delighted that people seem to like them. Since life is better with a little (or a lot of) magic, she writes urban fantasy and paranormal romance.

Linsey@LinseyHall.com
www.LinseyHall.com
https://twitter.com/HiLinseyHall
https://www.facebook.com/LinseyHallAuthor

ISBN 978-1-942085-44-7

Printed in Poland
by Amazon Fulfillment
Poland Sp. z o.o., Wrocław